LOVE AND DEATH
(Ai to Shi)

LOVE AND DEATH

(*Ai to Shi*)

by

SANEATSU MUSHAKOJI

Translated by

WILLIAM F. MARQUARDT

TWAYNE PUBLISHERS
New York

Copyright © 1958, by William F. Marquardt

Preface

It seems inevitable now that I would translate Saneatsu Mushakoji's *Ai to Shi* (Love and Death) some day. Being born of German immigrants made me a bilingual child and started me learning languages. World War II created the Navy Japanese Language School and started me learning Japanese. The reconstruction of Japan brought me five years later to Niigata University with the blessings of the Institute of International Education. There Professor Kingo Ochiai, head of the English department and close friend and disciple of Mushakoji, one of Japan's most beloved writers, soon had me working with him on *Love and Death,* Mushakoji's best known novel. Final link in the chain was the fact that after I returned to the States at the end of 1953 with only a rough draft, the story of the novelist Muraoka's shattered dreams and his peculiarly Oriental acceptance of his lot kept haunting me until I finally decided to share it with the American reader.

Besides Professor Ochiai, two other colleagues in the English department at Niigata University—Kenkichi Masutani and Sadayoshi Yokoo—had a hand in the translation. I worked with each of my three collaborators twice a week for two hours at a time, going over every sentence of Mushakoji's deceptively simple prose with them. These daily sessions made me sure-footed in my Japanese and confident of the accuracy of my interpretation, but, more important, they gave me insights into Japanese ways of thinking almost as valuable as those offered by the novel itself and were among my most satisfying experiences in Japan.

Between the first draft of the manuscript and the published book other hands also left their mark. From the author himself came permission to publish the translation of his novel and biographical data I had not found in any published source. Professors James W. Hall, Glenn H. Leggett, and S. K. Winther contributed stylistic suggestions. Professor Ichiro Awanuma of Meiji University checked the translation for accuracy. A less specific but nevertheless pervasive influence was the prodding, encouragement, and criticism of my wife.

Finally, I acknowledge with gratitude the grant from the Agnes H. Anderson Committee of the University of Washington which made the publication of this work possible.

Seattle, Washington
April, 1958

Introduction

Saneatsu Mushakoji has been translated into English before and in that respect is more fortunate than ninety-nine per cent of the writers of Japan who deserve attention. In 1930 an early one-act play of his, "A Family Affair," was translated by Glenn Hughes and Yozan Iwasaki. Three years later Noboru Hidaka translated another of his plays, "Aiyoku" (Passion). A third play was translated by Kiishi Nishi in 1935—"Sono Imoto" (His Younger Sister). In 1942 Moriaki Sakamoto translated his biography of Takamori Saigo, *The Great Saigo*.

These are all that we have in English of the works of a man who has published more than 500 in Japan and of whom a recent biographer said that the only day he failed to write or sketch during the entire war was the day he learned World War II was over.

For nearly 50 years Mushakoji has been a strong voice in Japan. He has made his impact in many forms—poetry, drama, novel, short story, essay, calligraphy, and sketching. His message has been essentially the same always: understand the individual human being, pity him, and make his lot better whenever the odds are against him.

Born in 1885 of noble parents, Mushakoji attended and graduated from the Peers School at the age of twenty-two. By this time his strong idealism had already manifested itself and disappointment in love had turned him to writing as an escape. As a student in the Peers School he had the effrontery to deliver a speech denouncing war in the presence of the great Russo-Japanese war hero, General Nogi, then president of the school.

After graduation from the Peers School, Mushakoji entered Tokyo Imperial University as a social science and literature student. Here he became an avid reader of Tolstoi and wrote his first published work, *Arano* (Wild Field) under his influence. Before long he also came under the influence of the teachings of Christ and Buddha. These three influences have been paramount in his writing throughout his life.

After only one year, Mushakoji left Tokyo University to devote all his time to writing. Gathering around him several young writers who were later destined for fame equal to his, he founded at the age of twenty-five a revolutionary magazine, *Shirakaba* (White Birch), dedicated to pointing up the crass materialism and the social inequalities of the newly arisen Japan. In its ten years' existence the magazine published some of the most vigorous writing of its day.

Not satisfied, however, with mere criticism of the evils he saw, Mushakoji attempted to put his ideals into practice. In 1918 he started in a village called Hyuga in Kyushu Prefecture a Japanese version of the Brook Farm experiment of the days of Thoreau and Hawthorne. In this Utopian community called *Atarashiki Mura* (New Village) the emphasis was to be on naturalness, spiritual growth, sharing of ownership, and equality of rights and responsibilities.

Unlike Brook Farm, New Village did not die of inanition. It has survived to the present day, though not on its original site. Commemorative issues on its fifteenth and thirtieth anniversaries in the village magazine testify to the vigor of the ideal which gave it birth. As recently as November 14, 1957 a letter from Mushakoji states that the 39th anniversary celebration of the founding of New Village was being held that very night in Mitaka-shi, a suburb of Tokyo.

Living in Utopia, however, did not spare Mushakoji some of the normal hazards of life. Married in 1913, he had had in his wife Fusako an enthusiastic supporter of his enterprises. She had worked hard with him to raise money and win members for the New Village project. But in 1922 Mushakoji fell in love with one of the members of the village, a young woman named Yasuko, and had a child by her. Fusako soon forgave her errant husband and agreed to an amicable divorce. Mushakoji then married Yasuko who in 30 years of marriage has borne him three daughters. Fusako also married again not long after the divorce.

An important event in Mushakoji's life, especially from the standpoint of the writing of *Love and Death,* was a seven months' trip he made in 1936 at the age of 52 to Europe. Like the novelist Muraoka in *Love and Death,* he traveled in France and Italy (and to several other countries not mentioned in *Love and Death),* studying masterpieces of painting and drama and noting the indifference of the West to the art and the people of the East.

Throughout his lifetime Saneatsu Mushakoji has represented unflagging affirmation of life. His humanitarianism, reverence for individuality, and belief in the brotherhood of man put him in harmony with the pacifism and social protest of the twenties and early thirties. With the increasing totalitarianism and chauvinism of the latter thirties and the war years, however, he was completely out of tune, and his popularity receded. The critic Yoshikazu Kataoka, writing in 1939—the year *Love and Death* was published—in *Introduction to Contemporary Japanese Literature,* said, "Today with the extinction of Individualism, [Mushakoji's outlook] is not, of course valued highly. Yet in spite of it, sentiments of respectful admiration are now and then voiced in the midst of uneasiness and perturbation that govern the world of thought—a realm wherein Marxism, as well as individualism, has been suppressed—for the settled state of mind achieved by the author."

The post-World War II era of American democracy and liberalism has brought Mushakoji into his own again. Since 1945 single works of his have been reprinted, collections of selected works edited by such literary greats as Naoya Shiga and Takeo Arishima have been published, and a huge 25-volume edition of his complete works has been launched.

Nor has his vein of creativity run out or lost appeal. A steady stream of essays, plays, poems, and stories continues to reach thousands of readers either as separate publications or as serials in popular periodicals. Titles such as *Ai to Jinsei* (Love and Life) (1947), *Kuso Sensei* (Sir Air Castle Builder) (1953), *Hana wa Mankai* (Flowers in Full Bloom) (1954), and *Bakaichi Banzai* (Hooray for Bakaichi) (1955) attest that his enthusiasm for living has not abated in the least.

Love and Death belongs to that familiar genre in Japan—the *shi-shosetsu* or I-novel. All novelists are to a great extent autobiographical, but whereas in America the novelist feels impelled to generalize or universalize his experiences so that they are no longer recognizable as his own, the Japanese genius for concentrating on the minute and the particular allows the Japanese novelist to exploit himself unabashedly as the hero of his novels.

The author of a *shi-shosetsu* does not, however, follow his own life-story slavishly. He takes a chunk of it and gives it whatever twist his fancy or his theme dictates. The travel experiences of Muraoka which fill so much of *Love and Death* are pure documentary, but they occurred not twenty but three years before in the life of the narrator. The love affair and the sad death of Natsuko are imaginary.

The year of publication—1939—is also significant for an understanding of the novel. Although, as has been pointed out, Mushakoji was not in tune with the prevailing mood of 1939, there are in *Love and Death* numerous concessions to popular feeling—the pointing up of the uniqueness of Japanese customs and dress, the querulousness about the indifference of the West to the importance of Japan, the resentment against the treatment accorded Orientals in Europe, the assertion of the equality of Eastern to Western art, the dwelling upon the satisfactions of travelling on a Japanese ship and being among Japanese again.

Despite these indications of Mushakoji's being carried along by the eddying whirlpool, *Love and Death* is a gloomy book for a man so unflaggingly affirmative in spirit. But what more appropriately premonitory title and theme for a novel published in 1939!

Mushakoji's concluding message that the living can get strength from realizing that the departed is in a more blessed state than he may be cheerless consolation for the Western reader. But we must remember that in the East *akirame*—resignation—has always been the chief imperative for living.

*T*HIS STORY took place twenty-one years ago. But it is one I cannot forget.

When I first called on Nonomura, I was twenty-five. I haven't forgotten the occasion even today.

At that time Nonomura was thirty but I thought of him as already a great man rather than merely a promising novelist. I feel that I was perhaps a bit foolish when I think about it now, but those were days when even a man of thirty could be a first-rate novelist, and Nonomura who had been famous at twenty-three or four was now at thirty on the threshold of greatness. At least so it seemed to me, a dedicated reader of Nonomura's works for some years.

Consequently I had pictured Nonomura as a far older man than he was. His youthfulness was quite a shock to me when I met him.

What led me to call on Nonomura was the fact that although the novels I had written up to that time were being criticized mercilessly, Nonomura, strangely enough, was always praising them. And so when I presented him a copy of my first published work as a token of gratitude, I received in return some very generous criticism and a note inviting me to come and have a chat with him whenever I was free.

And so, highly elated and at the same time slightly apprehensive, I paid him a call.

He was a man one felt at ease with at once. I still address him as Nonomura-san even today, but from that very first moment I knew in my heart that he was my friend, and he soon became a confidante to whom I unburdened myself of my most intimate thoughts without misgivings. I am fortunate to have in him one of those rare friends who is sympathetic no matter how unguardedly and thoughtlessly one talks.

2

Strangely enough, Nonomura found merit in me too. I don't want to suggest that he over-estimated me, but he praised me so much that others probably thought so, for he treated as my strong points the things others were condemning in me.

It is not my purpose to write about Nonomura. It is the fact that Nonomura's showing me more kindness than I deserved is one of the links in the chain of my story and not a desire to give the impression that I was unusually promising that impels me to make such a point of Nonomura's kindness. But I can't avoid mentioning that I was growing. If one is bothered too much by what irresponsible people think, one can't live purposefully.

I refuse to be so concerned about what my neighbors say that I become untrue to myself.

3

Whether out of eccentricity or perversity, Nonomura seemed given to admiring overly what others did not. At any rate, I came to like him and visited him occasionally. He was always glad to see me.

One day when I went to Nonomura's I saw several school girls playing in his garden. I was not especially interested but they were making a good deal of noise, so I stopped to look and saw two of them engaged in what looked like a handstand contest. One girl was clearly winning and was getting all the cheers.

"Incorrigible tomboy!" said Nonomura. I wondered what he was talking about. And I was surprised at the discovery that girls could be so frisky.

4

One day while going to Nonomura's I met at his gate a girl of seventeen or eighteen hardly past adolescence of slender figure and animated look.

Seeing me, she made a polite bow. There was in her features some resemblance to Nonomura, so I judged that she was Nonomura's younger sister and bowed politely in return. She then darted past me as if fleeing from something. Later I discovered that it *was* Nonomura's sister and the erstwhile winner of the handstand contest. Although I met her occasionally after that, I remember these two meetings most vividly.

For another two or three years, however, I was hardly aware of her presence. I heard people refer to Nonomura's younger sister as a beautiful girl, but it made no impression on me.

At times I noticed her beauty too, but, thinking that it had nothing to do with me, I did not allow myself to dwell on it. And because I seldom saw her and she was very young and really was nothing to me, I decided that I had better not think of the younger sister of my dear friend in an interested light.

Once Nonomura said, "My sister enjoys your works." But I gave little thought to this observation.

One or two years can do wonders to a person. Nonomura's sister blossomed into a very beautiful woman. When I met her on the street one day, she looked like a familiar and at the same time completely different person. I could hardly believe that this beautiful woman was Nonomura's sister. I was about to pass her without a word when she made a quick bow. Thinking she was bowing to someone else, I looked around, but seeing no one, I decided that she must be Nonomura's sister after all and returned her bow hastily. But she had already passed and I thought she had not seen my bow. I was sorry and rather disturbed.

About two months later I saw Nonomura's sister strolling in the Ginza with a few friends and I got ready to bow to her, but she passed without looking at me. I got the impression that I was being cut.

"Have it your own way!" was the thought that went through my mind. Struck by her beauty, I had hoped she would bow. I would never bow to her again! That was the childish resolve I made.

I was told later, however, that she had really not seen me that time. It was undoubtedly true, because when I met her a month or two later on my way to Nonomura's she bowed politely.

Pleased by this, I asked, "Is your brother at home?"

"Yes, he is."

We parted at this, but there's no denying that I was quite elated.

But I did not see her again for a long time. I had no special urge to see her. Then Nonomura's thirty-third birthday arrived. It was the twenty-fifth of February—a day I shall never forget.

5

On Nonomura's birthday it was customary for the young writers in Nonomura's circle to gather at his house and enjoy themselves in various parlor diversions. Since there were usually persons I did not particularly like in this gathering, I had decided not to go, but when the day came, for some reason I felt impelled to attend.

Five or six persons had already arrived when I got there and were talking animatedly. I joined the group and struck up a conversation with a few congenial spirits.

Soon it was announced that everybody was present and each person was given a seat in a large fifteen-mat room reserved for such gatherings. There were two lines facing each other running the length of the room. Nonomura's sister sat near one end and there were two or three women admirers present besides her.

Simple refreshments—sandwiches, rice-balls, cakes, and fruit—were brought out. Then saké was served. Since I do not drink saké I limited myself to eating. Soon the parlor diversions began. Everyone was required to make some sort of contribution and my turn was fast approaching. I was frightened at the thought of it and I made up my mind that I would definitely decline. The others were all talented, however, and no one was declining. And now finally it was my turn.

"I can't do a thing," I said, "so please let me off." But no one would hear of it. I blushed and became flustered. If there had been anything at all I could do I would surely have done it, but no matter how I wracked my brains, I could not think of a thing.

Then someone cried, "Why don't you squeal like a pig!" Everybody laughed.

The more flustered I became, the more I was taunted, especially by four or five persons who had not been very friendly to me for some time.

"Can't you just crawl on your hands and knees? No reason why you can't do that!"

"Oh, let's let him go!" urged Nonomura.

"No! No! We can't let him set a precedent for those whose turn is later." I grew more and more flustered. Perspiration began to appear on my forehead.

"Come on, get going!"

"None of these dignified airs now!" I became more and more incapable of acting. Suddenly Nonomura's sister interceded.

"Please let him off and let *me* do something instead!"

Everybody was startled at this offer from an unexpected quarter.

"May I?"

"You'll be more than satisfactory!"

"If you really think it's all right, I'll be glad to."

"A handstand!" someone cried. Everybody laughed.

Nonomura's sister got up and without hesitation ran out in front and turned a truly splendid aerial somersault. Everybody was dazzled by the unexpected brilliance of it and loud applause followed. When I thought of the load that had suddenly been lifted off my chest, I was so happy that my eyes grew moist.

Nonomura in his surprise exclaimed, "Hey Tomboy, when did you learn this?" Everybody laughed.

"Does it really matter when?" she retorted saucily and her expression struck me as being bewitchingly attractive. Everybody laughed.

"With your skill you could make a good living at that."

"Oh please, please!" she cried, pretending to glare at her brother.

Again everybody laughed. The tenseness in the atmosphere suddenly cleared and everybody was cheerful and animated again. Soon it was Nonomura's sister's turn. Someone called, "Another somersault, please!" But this time she remained demure and sang a song. This she also executed with real accomplishment and there was not the slightest suggestion of insincerity in the praise on everybody's lips.

From that time on I was not able to get Nonomura's sister out of my thoughts. And when I heard Nonomura call her "Nat-chan," I remembered that her name was Natsuko.

6

One day about ten days later, as I was on my way to Nono-
mura's, I suddenly came face to face with Natsuko herself.
We both bowed in friendly fashion. It was my first meeting with
Natsuko since Nonomura's birthday party.

"Thank you very much for helping me out the other day."

"I was afraid you were in trouble."

"I was never so paralyzed in all my life!"

"I was terribly nervous too. At that moment I was carried
away by a feeling of indignation, but afterwards I was worried whether you might not be angry at what I did, Sensei."

This first exchange of words with Natsuko made me very
happy. But I was annoyed at her calling me Sensei. Since I did
not know her very well yet, however, I could not bring myself
to protest against the form of address she used.

"Far from angry! You saved my life! Nothing ever made me
happier!"

"I'm relieved to hear you say that."

"I was really amazed at your skill at the somersault. It must
take a lot of practice to do it so well."

"It does. One day when a classmate of mine who had been
to a circus was describing a sensational aerial somersault she had
seen, I said even I could do that. Then she dared me to go
ahead and do it. When I seemed to hesitate, she was sure I
couldn't. But I had always been a tomboy and had loved doing
somersaults on the ground as a girl. That day simply by putting a little more energy into it I even managed to do a spin in
the air. Later I did it in front of my mother and was scolded
awfully for it. Finally she burst into tears and made me promise
never to do it again. 'What if you break your neck!' she said.
I didn't try it again until the other day, and in doing so I broke
my promise to my mother. With everybody so surprised and

so appreciative and I myself so elated at having carried it off,
I felt fine. Later that day, though, my mother took me in hand.
I was saved only when my brother came to my rescue and
my mother finally threw up her hands saying I was beyond hope,"
Natsuko ended, laughing.

Nonomura's house was nearer than it had ever seemed before.

7

Some time later I attended a play and Natsuko and her
brother and two or three of his friends were also there. It
seemed to me from a distance that she was chatting with her
usual cheerfulness.

I tried to look at her with indifference, but I had reached the
point where I could no longer be indifferent. Almost without
realizing it I had fallen in love with Natsuko. But she was not
bound to me; it was only I who was in love; Natsuko herself
felt nothing. Convinced that I would never be loved by any
woman, I had not allowed myself to think about her too much;
I had not tried to win her affection.

I also lacked confidence in my ability to create a home. Up
to now work had been everything to me. I had a burning
ambition to write something which Natsuko would not be able
to help admiring, but it was primarily an urge to assert my
power. I am rather ashamed to admit that when I was young
my desire to dominate was stronger than any other. Whenever
I was upset or unhappy about anything, I always tried to solve
my problem by my own efforts. My philosophy was that one
lived only to do good work. That is a most difficult philosophy
to bring to realization, but when I was young I did not know
that.

I believed that everything I saw and heard was a source of irritation and existed only to be controlled by me. I was jealous of any human being greater than myself. And my desire for stature was increasing. In Natsuko I recognized someone who had the power to advance my work, but I was ashamed to admit that she meant anything more than that.

Such an admission would have seemed to me immoderately selfish, a grasping for something beyond my reach.

I was determined to surpass even Nonomura. A tree whose branches obstruct the upward thrust of a growing tree must be pushed aside. I couldn't permit anyone to send his branches out over my head. My attitude somehow became quite obvious.

Nonomura, generous nature that he was, took on an expression which seemed to say that my attitude interested him and that he welcomed the idea of my surpassing him. This expression made me angry at times.

Nonomura was being hounded by all sorts of publishers for manuscript and his increasing income had given him extravagant tastes and he had to write far too much to satisfy them.

"Damned fool!" I couldn't help thinking. Yet when I read anything of his, I had to admit that he had quality. He had a beauty I couldn't equal. It had vastness—a certain greatness.

Compared to his my own writing seemed cramped.

"Pretty weak!" I had to admit.

But one must respect the greatness in the man who refuses to thrust another's head into the dirt but raises it aloft and breathes life into it.

I was quite enthusiastic about foreign novelists and admired them. But I couldn't hold back a desire to surpass even the greatest among them. The time was ripe for a great novelist to come out of Japan, I had written. I tried somehow to make myself believe that I myself was that long awaited novelist.

Reflecting about the matter now that I am along in years, I cannot delude myself into thinking I had been charmingly naive. I was really a hateful young fellow. But that is all over now.

8

Once Nonomura wrote the following words in an essay: "To have great confidence in oneself is a fine thing but to acquire it unnaturally by refusing to see the strong points in others is base. To give full recognition to the merit of another, to help him grow to the utmost of his capacity, and, after acknowledging fully his worth, to still have confidence in oneself—that is greatness. But a man lacking true self-confidence is apt to be satisfied with the momentary feeling of superiority which comes from denying merit in others and relentlessly pointing out their weaknesses."

Reading this, I blushed. I had the feeling that it was directed at me.

A bit nettled, I wrote the following thoughtless words: "True, a mountain does not have value simply from being tall, and a tree's worth does not lie in its capacity for attaining size. But a tree that has stopped growing undoubtedly consoles itself as it stands beside one that is still stretching upward with the thought that the other tree has little capacity for reflection. It cannot be demonstrated that there is any virtue in mere bigness, but the high mountain looking at a low mountain cannot help thinking that the other is lower than itself."

From Nonomura came the following letter: "In criticizing persons with excessive self-confidence, I wasn't referring to you.

I have always taken pride in the respect you pay me. The fact that you seem to take my words as an attack on yourself makes me feel that you do not trust the strength of my friendship and my faith in you. But it hurts me to have given you even a little displeasure. Please don't put off coming over to my place for a chat. My sister has become a dedicated reader of yours of late. She's always asking why you haven't been coming."

I lost no time calling on Nonomura. He was very happy to see me.

"A tree that has stopped growing is, as you say, a pathetic thing," he observed rather cheerfully.

"Deep in my heart, I don't believe that fits you!"

"Probably not a direct hit, but you didn't miss by far. From now on I'll try to be a bit more steady," he said. Natsuko happened to be out.

9

That night I dreamed I was at a vaudeville show.

Natsuko came on stage dressed as a clown, did handstands, and turned somersaults in the air. Then she looked at me and smiled. There was something strangely fascinating about her and when I awoke I couldn't put her face out of my mind.

I didn't mention this to a soul.

10

Two or three days later I went to Nonomura's, but Nonomura was out. Just as I was about to leave Natsuko appeared.

"My brother should be back shortly. Won't you please come in and wait?" she said.

I accepted her invitation and went in. Natsuko herself brought the tea and cakes.

"I've been assigned to keeping an eye on the house today," she said.

"Is Nonomura-san due back soon?"

"I don't know."

"You just said he was."

"If I hadn't, Sensei, you would have left. So I told a little lie. Anyhow I really think he will be back quite soon. He's awfully unpredictable though, and he has many friends, so you can't depend on him. But he'd be very angry, Sensei, and would scold me for not holding you, if I let you go. I've been telling my sister-in-law that men certainly are selfish."

"Aren't women a little more selfish too than we are in the habit of thinking?"

"When one is never held to account for what he does, he is bound to become selfish. My brother has no one whose wishes he needs to consider, and so he is becoming more and more selfish."

"Isn't there anyone Nonomura-san is in awe of?"

"One person. Do you know who?"

"Your late father?"

"No."

"Your mother?"

"No."

"Someone living?"

"Yes."

"Someone in Japan?"

"Yes. Now do you know who?"

"No I don't."

"Someone right here."

I was dumfounded, but I feigned innocence and said, "Is it you?"

"Now you don't believe that," Natsuko laughed coquettishly. "Strangely enough, it's you my brother is afraid of."

"Are *you*?"

"I don't really know you."

"I respect your brother very much."

"You do?"

"I really do."

"From the bottom of your heart?"

"Yes."

"Don't you feel just a bit superior to him too?"

"Not at all!"

"My brother said you do. He says you have a strange power, but he's not certain whether you will reveal yourself best in literature or in some other form."

"What he is saying is self-revelation. People are always talking about themselves. But I do confess to a fear of remaining an immature writer all my life. I hope that ultimately my innermost being will be embodied in words, but whether I have what it takes to realize that hope, I don't know."

"My brother once said something to this effect: 'I'm pinning my faith on the last human being. He will be the realization of what we have been aspiring to. But this is only a flickering vision.' "

"If Nonomura-san really has such a vision, he's indeed a lucky fellow."

"He seems to think at times as you do. Once he expressed himself something like this: 'I should hate to be the last human. Unless he were ten thousand times wiser or ten thousand times more stupid than I he would probably lose his mind with no other person to talk to. Only a completely apathetic being would be able to get along in such a state of things.' When someone asked how he would manage to get his food, he laughed and said that by that time people would be able to convert air or water or plants or sand into food and would be able to eat without exerting themselves in the least."

"How would you like to be the last human?"

"That would be awful!"

"What do you think of the present?"

"I have never thought about any other time."

"You are in the happiest time of life."

"Why do you say that?"

"Because the world is full of the things you love."

"I think I am now in the worst time of life."

"Why?"

"I'm like a ship without an anchor. I think I'd rather be an actress or a paid entertainer."

"What does Nonomura-san say to that?"

"If I had no interest in marriage he probably wouldn't object. But he doesn't like to be involved in anyone else's problems. 'I don't want to exercise authority over you,' he says, 'but I won't be responsible for what happens to you if you go ahead with it.' In short, he seems opposed to the idea."

"I was under the impression that you are at the height of happiness."

"Why do you say that?"

"I thought you'd surely have a sweetheart."

"Would that were true!" said Natsuko with a light laugh.

"Is it because you're too hard to satisfy?"

"With such an excellent chance to study my brother's married life, you see, I feel that I understand the realities of marriage only too well."

"Nonomura-san's wife seems to be a very fine person."

"She's too good! And so he goes out whenever he pleases. Nevertheless, he doesn't strut in front of my sister-in-law. When he's home he's always trying to please her. Of course, he gets cross occasionally. And my sister-in-law sometimes treats my brother like a fool and she complains to him. Yet she is in awe of him and keeps prudently quiet in all the important matters. They don't seem to be especially close to each other. And yet when they get intimate they are very much so. But they cool off very soon. When one sees marriage as it really is one can't help being disillusioned."

"But isn't there something rather satisfying about it too that we don't quite grasp?"

"I haven't been able to detect very much that is satisfying. . . . Well, talk about the Devil and he's sure to appear! Here they both come!" said Natsuko, hurrying out to meet them.

I was sorry I couldn't talk longer to Natsuko. It was not the subject matter that pleased me so much as the fact that the conversation was carried on in such a leisurely manner. And I confess that it gave me great pleasure to look at Natsuko's beautiful face and figure, her animated features, and her graceful movements. And somehow I had the feeling at times that our spirits were attuned to each other. To put it more plainly, I was now hopelessly in love with Natsuko.

11

I am not certain whether the fact that humanity has the gift of love means greater happiness or unhappiness for the individual. To anyone in love, however, love seems to be the only reality. I was now at the stage where awake or asleep Natsuko was never out of my mind.

Without my realizing it, Natsuko was undermining all my bachelor instincts. I called on Nonomura more and more frequently, and whenever he was away I always hoped that Natsuko would come flying out to meet me.

Things do not always turn out as we hope. But sometimes when we feel most that things are not going well they may, without our being aware of it, be shaping themselves to suit our desires.

One day one of my poet-friends called to tell me that he was thinking of publishing a volume of poetry and was planning to raise the necessary money by putting on a sort of literary benefit show and wanted to know if I would mind saying a few words at it. I immediately consented; whereupon he asked if I didn't know someone talented enough at singing or dancing to provide some entertainment at the same time.

I didn't know anyone, I said, but suddenly the image of Nonomura's sister Natsuko floated through my mind. If only Natsuko would agree to it, I thought, she could certainly put on a fine show. I was thinking more in terms of how much *I* would enjoy seeing her than of how much others might. Then I told my friend that I knew someone who was not trained in singing or dancing but could put on a novel show and that I would be happy to ask her if she would do it. He said that he would not be able to offer any payment. I replied that she was not likely to want any.

He then asked what sort of show she would put on, but I answered with an air of mystery that I couldn't say just now.

"I'd really appreciate your asking her," my friend said.

"I'm not sure she'll agree, but I'll ask her," I replied.

After my friend's departure I wrote Natsuko a letter.

12

"I am writing this letter to ask a favor of you. This is a strange request and I'm afraid it may offend you, but I have been in a frame of mind of late in which I dare to ask you anything. If this request is improper, I give you leave to be angry with me, but I hope you will forgive me. This is the situation. A poet-friend, Mr. O., wants to publish a volume of poetry, and, since he lacks funds, he plans to raise some money with a literary benefit show. He asked me to say a few words and also to help him find some interesting entertainment for the occasion. I hope you won't be angry when I confess that you popped into my head at that moment. I didn't mention your name or the sort of entertainment. I said merely that I knew someone who would be able to provide some novel entertainment but wasn't sure whether she would be willing to do so and I promised to try to get her. Please don't be angry! It's really your fault. I was so startled and charmed by your gracefulness, that I have become obsessed with a desire to see it again. I really won't mind your refusing. Please don't say anything about this when we see each other again."

From Natsuko immediately came the following reply.

"I was very much surprised to receive your letter. When I read it, I was first dumbfounded and then so amused I had to laugh. Whether I should consent or not I leave for you to decide, Sensei. If you really want to see me do a somersault, I will do it whenever you wish. But the only good thing about it is its novelty. I seldom do it for an audience. I will do whatever you command, Sensei."

In high spirits, I replied as follows:

"Your letter gave me pleasure, but I was somewhat embarrassed by your addressing me as Sensei. I've been intending for some time, if the chance ever came, to ask you not to. I am also disturbed at your saying that I should command you. But I happen to be in the mood for shocking people. My friend would be delighted to have you keep your identity secret indefinitely and do your act incognito. I'm sure no one would recognize you if you disguised yourself as a clown or as a boy. I will tell my friend that you have agreed to do it.

"You may be angry when I tell you this, but I dreamed some time ago that I saw you on the stage in a vaudeville show dressed as a clown turning somersaults. The way you looked is still fresh in my memory."

There was an immediate reply from Natsuko:

"Thank you for your letter. I promise not to call you Sensei on condition that you stop thinking of me in connection with somersaults. But if you persist in talking about somersaults I will keep calling you Sensei.

"I will be delighted to do what you request. But I can't for the life of me see how my doing a somersault or a handstand would be very interesting. I am, after all, only an amateur. I could never hope to match the performance of the professionals. I may give my dear Sensei a little pleasure, but the public will hardly take notice of me. So I suggest, Sensei, that we get together and work out a short skit into which we will put as many somersaults and handstands as you can stand seeing. I could get together with one of my friends who is good at comedy and work out something. I'm afraid that if I put on too silly a show, it will reflect on you, Sensei, and I hope you will forgive me. Your being capable of the dream you described, Sensei, has completely disillusioned me about your character, but my revenge will be your disillusionment when you see it come true. Your friend will certainly be disappointed. But since it is you, my dear Sensei, who will bear the responsibility, I am not the least bit concerned whether your friend is pleased or not. I won't mind using an assumed name. But my own name would be all right too. You needn't be so fastidious on that point, Sensei.

"My brother once wrote that human beings were neither born to be laughed at nor not to be laughed at, and you yourself, Sensei, wrote somewhere, didn't you, that being skilled at something now is better than having once been skilled, and that having once been inept does not mean that one will always be inept. I agree. Now please keep in mind that I'm not a professional acrobat, my dear Sensei, Sensei, Sensei."

Reading this last, I made a grimace. But, of course, I wasn't really offended. I looked forward eagerly to the appointed day.

13

The day came at last.

I and two others spoke in praise of my friend's poetry. My friend read some of his poetry to the gathering and then the entertainment followed. After some singing and dancing, Natsuko's act was announced under the title "Tomboy." As the time for Natsuko's appearance approached, my feeling of elation gave way to one of acute discomfort. I felt a bit ashamed and decided that I would have been far better off if I had never been asked to be connected with this silly bsuiness.

I even questioned whether Natsuko's readiness to give her consent wasn't a bit brazen.

But time moved on relentlessly. The singing and dancing were faultless, being the contribution of professionals. But since until now all the performers had been males, the audience was ready for something more colorful and applauded vigorously when the title of the act was announced. The more they applauded the more ashamed I felt and I offered a silent prayer that she would carry it off.

The curtain went up with the beat of a drum. I had no idea what the plot would be. A woman in the role of a mother began a chant. She was interrupted by a loud bang backstage.

"At it again! Was there ever a girl so exasperating!" exclaimed the mother. Just as she was about to resume her chant, there was another sound as of something falling.

"Haruko, Haruko! What in the world are you doing?" cried the mother.

From back-stage came the voice of Natsuko, "I'm not doing anything, it's only the mice squealing."

"You mean to tell me that the mice are squealing now?"

Through a partly open sliding door appeared the face of Natsuko, saying, "Oh yes they are. Whenever you begin to sing the mice caper madly. Awfully spooky, isn't it?"

Natsuko's face was made up to be funny, but it was strangely beautiful.

"None of your foolishness now! It's three o'clock, you know. Time for your koto practice."

"Yes, Mother," said Natsuko, picking up the koto leaning against the wall and beginning to pluck it. She played beautifully and everybody was lost in admiration. Then the mother said, "I've got a few things to do, so I'm going out. Now you be a good girl while I'm away. Don't you do any of your handstands or somersaults the minute I'm out as you did last time."

"But Mother I've got to be in a handstand match with one of my friends on the twentieth. If I lose, I'll have to treat them all to black tea."

"Isn't it a rather small matter, even if you do have to serve them black tea?"

"But there'll be an awful lot of persons."

"A lot? How many?"

"At least fifty."

"Fifty!" exclaimed the mother toppling backwards from the shock.

"Well, I . . . I promised to treat all the kids in my class."

"You did what? . . . Oh but surely you'll win."

"I think I should too, but my opponent's awfully good. She can walk about twenty-four yards on her hands."

"And you?"

"I ordinarily do about twenty yards."

"Then you might lose, mightn't you?"

"But the other girl can't do the somersault. So I'll come out all right even if I do walk two yards less."

"You'll come out all right? Do you think so?"

"It'll be close though. The other girl's mother is an expert at the handstand and coaches her every day. Just the opposite of the way things are here. So it's quite possible for me to lose."

"That would be awful! In that case you'd better let the koto go and practice the handstand. Fifty persons! How terrible!"

"If I practice hard from now on, I'll do all right."

"All right then, start practicing! What are you standing around for? Get going!"

"I'll get ready right away." She went out.

Mother: "Fifty persons, fifty! What a crazy promise to make! I'd better get going myself!" She put a cloth around her head and began to clean up the room.

Natsuko came out wearing silk slacks. I was struck by her beauty in them also. I was no longer ashamed. She was remarkably graceful and I was thrilled at the unrestrained laughter of the audience.

When the time came for her to do the handwalk, however, I felt tense again, but Natsuko walked along on her hands quite unconcernedly. Whenever she did well, the mother clapped her hands shouting, "Fine! Fine!" but whenever Natsuko stopped or faltered, she cried, "Come on now! Come on now!" Everybody laughed. Natsuko was performing with perfect ease and composure.

"Is she a professional?" my poet-friend asked.

"Not in the least. She's strictly amateur."

Two or three persons in the audience had recognized her as Nonomura's sister and were proudly informing the others, but except for these two or three, the audience evinced nothing but interest and amusement. When she finished at last, she exclaimed, "Oh, I'm all in!"

"You must be burning up!" the mother said, waving a fan in her face. "Do you really think you'll win? It'll be just too bad, if you lose. That was certainly a silly wager to make. Your opponent's family must be worried too."

"But they're millionaires."

"Heavens! How in the world did you get to take on someone like that?"

"Well, I thought I'd win. She was awfully conceited and a certain sly miss was egging me on, saying that with her being so cocky about her handstand we might get her to treat us all by challenging her to a match. I was carried away by the suggestion and agreed to the scheme. Well, the girl egging me on happened to be one of my opponent's spies."

"That's what comes of foolish bragging. This month would be an especially bad time for you to lose. Next month we could manage somehow."

"Don't worry. I won't lose, even if it kills me!"

"How would it be if you withdrew?"

"But I'm a woman! It would be disgraceful for a woman's pledge to prove less sacred than a man's."

"Then you insist on going through with it?"

"I certainly do!"

"Well if you're going ahead with it, put up a good fight!"

"I'll do my very best!"

"You say this girl can't do an aerial somersault?"

"They say she's been practicing hard lately, so she probably can now."

"That's terrible! Can you?"

"I think so, but I'm not sure. I haven't done one since you scolded me for it."

"Try one now."

"May I?"

"Of course!"

"All right then, I will." Natsuko then did a quick somersault.

"Wonderful! Wonderful!" exclaimed the mother, clapping her hands.

I'm not sure whether they had been planted in the audience or not, but a group of women began to laugh loudly and to clap their hands in unison. Then the curtain came down.

It was a trivial thing, but there was something charming and pretty about it. I applauded loudly too.

Next came singing again. People were still whispering about Natsuko's beauty, her innocence, and her gracefulness. I rather expected Natsuko to come before long and chat with me.

But she never came. After the singing was over, I went backstage, but she had already left. My poet-friend expressed his thanks. He assured me that everybody had been most delighted with the skit. Then I learned that Natsuko had left with about ten women and three or four men who had gathered backstage right after the performance. They had taken her somewhere to drink a toast in her honor.

This news stirred me to jealousy. I could not believe she could be so flighty. Also, her allowing herself to be toasted for such a trifling feat made her sink in my esteem. All the joy I had felt until now vanished. When I got home, I had the urge to write a note of protest, but I put the thought aside as being rather childish. Then three or four days later I got a letter from Natsuko. This is what my heart had been waiting for. I opened it quickly.

"Forgive me for my conduct the other day. I am deeply depressed over the fact that my miserable performance has probably turned you against me, Sensei. I wanted very much to see you that evening for I needed your consolation, Sensei, but my friends dragged me away and, besides, I was a bit afraid too to see you because I was ashamed. I'm glad the whole business is over. The way I feel now, I would hate anyone who ever asked me to do such a thing again. My friends assured me that I did well and were kind enough to drink a toast in my honor, but I felt strangely lonely and wanted very much to cry. I'm waiting for your letter, Sensei, no longer my sensei. Please forget this foolish business."

Upon finishing the letter I was ashamed of the petty resentment I had been cherishing against her. I felt that I deserved to be punished severely for harboring it.

Then I quickly wrote a letter in reply.

"Your letter gave me real pleasure. I'm really the one to apologize. But if you had been conceited about your performance I might have been disappointed in you. Before your act began I was in a cold sweat, but the more I watched you the prouder I became. The plot was silly, but you and your friend were far from silly. What I longed to see and to let others see is your great beauty, which you seem to be not aware of—though perhaps you are. I felt strangely as if I myself had written the skit and also as if I had produced it. If you have been even slightly unhappy about your performance, I am to blame. I, for one, was thrilled by it. What bothered me most, though, was the thought going through my mind that someone else might be even more thrilled than I.

"It is I who should be begging *your* pardon. I wanted to congratulate you in private. But when I learned that while I was trying to summon up courage to walk out on the singing, other persons less agitated and more daring had showered you with praises, I lost my desire to say anything to you. I decided to keep silent until I saw you again. It's really too late now for me to thank you.

"All my friends who saw you perform thought you were wonderful. I was amazed at your handstands and somersaults. But from now on I promise to refrain from uttering the word 'somersault' on condition you stop calling me 'Sensei.' I'm planning to call on you some afternoon one of these days. Please give my regards to Nonomura-san."

14

The very next afternoon I went to Nonomura's house. Nonomura was out but Natsuko met me at the door.

"Well, hello there! I was wondering whether you would call today."

"And Nonomura-san?"

"I really don't know where he is. He's been out a lot lately, and my sister-in-law is worried. She's afraid my brother's misbehaving."

"Oh, I doubt that."

"Men aren't very trustworthy."

"Aren't you a bit too severe now?"

"But my father, my uncle, and seven out of every ten other men I know can't be trusted."

"Oh come now, I'd say there aren't more than three out of ten of us who can't be trusted."

"You really believe that? I thought I was being generous when I said seven out of ten. I wanted to say nine out of ten. I mean men who are truly faithful husbands."

"A gross exaggeration! It may apply to the bourgeosie, but not to men who work for a living."

"But practically every man I know is always boasting about his silly affairs. My mother and aunt both seem to think there is nothing they can do about it. Besides, the world seems to have been arranged for the convenience of men who want to do such things. And so I don't consider my brother exceptionally wicked, but when I think of my sister-in-law, I can't help disliking what my brother is doing. My sister-in-law is such a fine person."

"But you don't need to worry about Nonomura-san."

"Is he dependable though? My brother is good-natured enough, but he's a bit selfish too. My sister-in-law never complains and so he doesn't seem to realize that he is making her unhappy. But isn't it stupid of him not to see that? So I took it upon myself one day to say to him, 'My dear brother, you don't seem to be yourself these days.' 'Am I different than usual?' he said. 'Haven't you made a new friend?' I said. 'I have lots of friends.' 'That's not what I mean.' 'They're all the same to me.' 'But several persons have said they see you frequently out walking with someone.' 'Anything wrong with walking with someone?' my brother asked. 'How brazen!' I said. Then he asked whether I had said anything to my sister-in-law. When I said I hadn't, he laughed and said, 'Don't tell her then. If she understood the real circumstances, you see, she wouldn't mind.' What a wicked way to talk!"

"I think Nonomura-san may be telling the truth. If we only knew the real circumstances everything would probably be quite all right. We tend to keep relations between men and women secret, but if we kept them out in the open, there would probably be little in them that would seem shocking."

"How can you say such a thing!"

"You're really quite naive. Don't you realize that Nonomura moves in a world different from yours? Nevertheless, that 'friend' may some day not be so impersonal toward Nonomura-san, and even though *he* intends to carry on his friendship without becoming emotionally involved, *she* may not be able to. I don't deny that these things are annoying, but I believe Nonomura-san is quite dependable."

"Then you don't disapprove of him?"

"Not at all."

"You and my brother are two of a kind, aren't you, Sensei?"

"You don't understand such matters yet, but you seem to love your brother very much."

"That's why I get angry at him. He hasn't always been like this."

"Your feeling that everybody should be good and never make anyone unhappy is naive. So you mustn't get angry at him. You should have faith in him."

"I never expected this of you, Sensei."

"Nonomura-san is wiser than you."

"Wiser, perhaps! But I'd call it craftier!"

"What do you mean by that?"

"You and my brother are birds of a feather. You'll stand by him no matter what."

"You'd better have faith in him. You're silly not to . . ."

"Silly, you say . . . ?"

"You don't understand the male point of view."

"I thoroughly despise that point of view!"

"Just the same, Nonomura-san is a trustworthy man. You'd better stay out of his affairs. This is your sister-in-law's concern, so you'd better not cause any unnecessary trouble."

"Unnecessary, you say!" exclaimed Natsuko staring me in the face. Then suddenly smiling, she said, "Now that you put it that way, it does seem a bit unnecessary."

"It's easy to understand your being angry," I conceded.

"I can't help loving my brother very much. That's why I want him to be fine and above reproach."

"You always try to get just what you want, don't you?"

"Do you really have faith in my brother, Sensei?"

"I certainly do. You can always depend upon a man who is never petty or malicious."

"Even when he causes someone pain?"

"Nonomura-san will never deliberately do anything to cause someone pain. But he is inclined to be self-centered and to have no thought for the present."

"That's just it! And he doesn't care one bit what I think or say."

"If he had faults that he could correct merely by following your advice, he would have corrected them long ago."

"Today you are really playing teacher, Sensei."

"I find it easier and easier to talk to you."

"You mean you're getting to see more clearly what a foolish person I am."

"There may be something in what you say."

"That skit we put on *did* have a silly plot."

"It was clever enough, but sort of trivial. Who wrote it?"

"I did with some help from my friend."

"Whose idea was it to open with the koto?"

"My friend's. I objected to the koto part because I'm awful on the koto, but when she insisted that that would be all the better, I brazenly went ahead with it."

"I'm hardly an authority, but I thought you were very good."

"My brother scolded me for not letting him know that I was going to do it. But I replied, 'I kept it from you because I would have been ashamed to have you see it.' 'That answer deserves a passing grade,' he said. 'I would have been too ashamed to go and see you. Not being told beforehand was a real blessing.' "

"It turned out all right. I had worried some though. Did you go anywhere afterwards?"

"Yes, I went out for tea with a group, but I had a strange feeling of loneliness, so I insisted before long on leaving them and going home. They were disappointed and said that in that case they would all go home. Then they broke up and went their separate ways. Then feeling a strange urge to see you, Sensei, I slipped back to the meeting hall, but not a soul was there. So I went home feeling I wanted to have a good cry."

"That was too bad. I wanted to see you just as badly that night."

We both suddenly looked up into each other's eyes and smiled. It was as if we had caught a glimpse of each other's heart.

15

Humanity has been blessed with many kinds of happiness. And I was now slave to one of the greatest of happinesses. Natsuko had become a being indispensible to me. By merely sending a card I could summon her anywhere I happened to be. And whenever I received a card from Natsuko with some request I would drop everything to grant it.

Wherever Natsuko was I was, and wherever I, Natsuko. But we had never mentioned marriage. It was as if the matter had once been decided and we were afraid to bring it up again. Nonomura gave his tacit consent. I was in the heights of ecstacy.

But on the journey of life the road opens and closes at unexpected times. At this juncture I was invited by my uncle in Paris to visit him there. I had once written my uncle that I would like to see Paris. But I had forgotten about it completely. Now here was this uncle for some unaccountable reason asking if I wouldn't like to come to Paris. Just now I had no desire to go, and I decided to refuse. But I disliked keeping anything secret from Natsuko, so I went to her and told her about it.

Whereupon Nonomura said, "By all means go. If you don't go now, you may never get to go. It would be worth going merely for the sights you'll see." Then he looked hard at Natsuko and continued, "You agree, don't you? It would be for Muraoka's (my name) own good."

"I don't know."

"What do you mean, you don't know?"

But Natsuko said nothing.

"I don't care very much to go," I said.

"I think you'd better go. You won't have to stay long. Going for a half year or even a year wouldn't hurt anything," said Nonomura.

"If it's only for a half year, it'll be all right. I'll spend the time you're away on some useful studies," Natsuko said suddenly with a deep blush.

"If it's all right with you, I'll go," I said forthrightly.

Nonomura left without a word. As soon as her brother was gone, Natsuko ran to me. "Please don't forget me!" she implored.

"Don't *you* forget *me!* Will you marry me when I get back?"

"Yes."

It was our first mention of marriage.

"I'd like to go with you."

"It'll be lonesome going without you."

"You must see everything and then tell me about it when you get back."

"I will. But to tell the truth, I don't want to go."

"As for me, when I think of the miserable half year ahead . . . But you must go for the sake of your future."

"I don't think it's as important as all that."

To be perfectly honest, I did want to go. But I had been seized by the fear that while I was away someone might come and take Natsuko away. Now I was confident that such a thing could never happen.

But even as this thought came to me I had the feeling that I ought not tempt fate.

But it was unthinkable not to trust Natsuko. It would be all right to go, I decided.

But however trustworthy Natsuko was, fate was not.

16

I was now committed to making the trip to the West. From now on I saw Natsuko every day.

We talked a great deal about how happy we would be after I returned. We toyed with the notion that we might actually enjoy the loneliness of separation, but we also asked ourselves what we would do when the desire to see each other became unbearable.

I was young. I had all sorts of strange notions about the West. I couldn't help dreaming of what I would do if I were rich, but I believed that even without being rich I could grow and win the sort of happiness money could not buy.

One moonlight night, we took a walk along the beach. Not a soul was out besides us. Natsuko had quietly adopted the familiar *you* in talking to me.

"I have made up my mind that I can endure anything for the sake of the great work you will do some day. My brother has given me all sorts of advice. Recently he said to me, 'Pleasure is not the goal of life.' I wanted to say, 'Why don't you adopt that principle yourself?' But I'm sure what my brother says is right. I have learned that one's duty in life, however austere, must come before pleasure."

"You're to be admired. I too must try to learn the meaning of duty."

" 'He who has not wandered in the valley of loneliness or of tears has not learned of life.' I wonder who said that."

"I know a passage something like it, but it's not quite so insipid."

"Well, let me hear it then."

"I seem to have forgotten it. But I'm sure it was more impressive than that."

"Perhaps it was . . . I've been too irresponsible up to now. From now on I'm really going to learn how to run a home. I'm going to study cooking very hard while you're away so that you can have good things to eat every day after you get back."

"Won't that cost money?"

"Are you worrying about money already?"

"But I want to live a life of self-denial."

"You're a strange man!"

"Do you think you're up to it?"

"Of course I am! But if I weaken, I'll slip off to my father's now and then for dinner."

"That's the spirit! But if you get too accustomed to doing things on the sly, I may live to regret it."

"That applies to me too."

"Isn't this a bit early for a family squabble?"

"You're the one who's doing it. You're making the insinuations."

"Come now, let's try to be more sensible!"

"All right, let's!"

"It's wonderful luck for me to have met you. I want very much to marry you as soon as I get back. I intend to pick up all sorts of things on the trip for our home. My uncle seems to favor me more than his other nephews. It may be because my father died when I was very young. On his deathbed my father said to my uncle, 'If this boy gets a good education, he will make something of himself,' and he pleaded with him to look after me. My uncle once told me that those words have never faded from his memory. He probably invited me because he happened to have my father on his mind of late."

"A truly generous man, your uncle! Isn't he?"

"Just now an uncle with unwanted gifts!"

That was all there was to it, I believed. But I learned later that he had received a letter from my mother expressing worry about my becoming so deeply involved with Natsuko and so the truth undoubtedly was that his invitation was a form of meddling. That possibility had not occurred to me. I would certainly have declined if it had. Natsuko had not suspected anything either when she had remarked, "A truly generous man, your uncle." He was a good uncle but also an officious one.

"You'll be punished for talking like that. I'm really happy for your sake. When I think of the day of your return I forget all thoughts of the loneliness I will endure until then because of what I have to look forward to. By the time you get back I shall have made myself worthy of being your bride. So please bring back all kinds of lovely things for me!"

"Here! Here! You know I would even if you ordered me not to."

"Don't then!"

We both laughed. Time passed without our being aware. Suddenly we realized that there was a full moon high in the heavens. We were hardly conscious of our surroundings or the sound of the waves. But it was high time we were getting back.

"Shall we start back?"

"Yes. I'll never forget this night."

"I certainly shall never forget."

Even now I haven't forgotten, though this happened twenty-one years ago.

17

Three days before my departure for the West, a small group of persons came together to give me a farewell party. It was held in Nonomura's guest room. There were only twenty persons present. It was a very friendly gathering. Natsuko attended to the guests cheerfully and unobtrusively.

Someone called out teasingly, "In the mood for a somersault?"

"Not at all," was Natsuko's demure reply.

Nonomura gave the first of the farewell speeches. "I was the first to urge Muraoka to go to Paris," he said. "Thousands and ten thousands have gone and will continue to go. There is nothing spectacular about making the trip. But Paris is the cultural center of the world today. I would like to have him learn from his trip how frivolous the world really is. What I got from the literature course in Tokyo Imperial University in the way of knowledge I could have gotten by reading a single volume, but an important thing I did get was a point of view which spares me from being the least bit impressed by the reputation of that most noble seat of learning. That point of view, I might say, has given me awareness and self-confidence. From the standpoint of knowledge, one would be better off reading a book than going to Europe or Paris. But the awareness that Europe or Paris are frivolous places is something one can get only by going to the West. And that, I maintain, is not at all an insignificant possession. Paris is not the center of the world; it is wherever we happen to be standing. Let us think about the fact that the earth is round. For us the center of the earth is Tokyo. To live decently is the most important thing of all for us. But until we have seen Paris we remain in awe of Paris. That Paris is nothing to be in awe of is the feeling that Muraoka will come back with and he will realize that it is a good thing for us to be proud and to do the work that we consider right. Read all the books you want—after you come back. I want Muraoka to strive for general impressions—to probe with his sharp insight into the minds of the people of Paris. After he has gained a new self-awareness, I want him to come back and work with a new spirit. What we expect of him is not travelogues but growth in self-knowledge and self-confidence. A half year from now we will be giving him a welcome home party in this same room. I am already thrilled at the thought of that meeting, and so I send Muraoka off now with a distinct feeling of pleasure. Let's drink to Muraoka's successs!"

Nonomura raised his glass. The others did likewise. When I turned to look at Natsuko, she was looking at me. We smiled at each other without anyone's noticing. I touched glasses with the person next to me, but it was really my heart touching Natsuko's.

After two or three others had spoken, I was called upon to say something too. "I'm grateful to you all," I began, "for sending me off in such good spirits and with such high hopes for me. But I myself don't understand too clearly why I am going. It may be simply a case of 'travel at company—I should say, uncle's—expense.' As Nonomura has said, I don't think I will get much out of a half year's visit. As you all know, I have no talent for learning foreign languages. To get even a general idea of the contents of the simplest book, I have to read it two or three times. And French I don't know at all. So I'll be pretty much limited to looking at painting and sculpture and staring at people. I probably won't learn much about food or music either. But I will learn something. I don't know just what, but Jesus said that there is one thing needful and I think I can learn that one thing. I mean to say, I'm confident I can study the wordless whisperings of people's

hearts and the invisible life of the city. Any activity that re-
quires more than proficiency in Japanese will be pretty much
closed to me. Knowledge that I can't get through Japanese will
be lost to me. I'm sorry to say I will have to see things primarily
through Japanese eyes. Nonomura-san has said it is good
that the earth is round. I'm of the same opinion. I think the
best place for a Japanese to study the literature of other countries is Japan. On that Nonomura-san and I are also in agree-
ment. But I want to see and come to understand Paris and
other places as much as possible. I want to learn everything
that is worth learning before I come back. But Nonomura-san,
after all, probably knows me better than anyone. Nonomura-san
has the gift of being able to perceive without undertaking such
a trip what I cannot unless I do. If after half a year away
I return safely, what joy it will be to see you all here again.
I'm a man who leaves home just for the pleasure of coming
back."

Everybody laughed. I finished and sat down. Everybody
clapped. Nonomura looked at me and smiled as if he had
glimpsed my innermost thoughts. Natsuko glanced at me shyly
and smiled.

Those who liked saké drank. Natsuko sang a short song.
She sang very beautifully.

18

I saved the day before my departure for Natsuko.

She was waiting for me when I arrived at the Tokyo Station.

Contrary to her usual practice, she was wearing kimono. She
wanted me to have a vivid final impression of Japan, she
explained. Besides, I would be seeing many beautiful women
in Western style dresses from now on. I'm no judge of clothes,

but she certainly looked more bewitching than ever before. Her spirits, however, seemed somewhat more subdued than usual.

Realizing that we would not see each other for some time, I was eager to have my last memory of her as beautiful and satisfying as possible.

About two hours later we found ourselves in a detached cottage at a hotel on the Shonan beach. Although we liked walking, the early May sun was already too hot for any sort of exertion. Besides, we were tired. Getting ready for a trip to the West is fatiguing.

My mother was constantly worried that she was not taking care of things well enough for me. She seemed happy enough about my going. But as the time of departure approached she worried more and more, and, since it did her no good to talk to me about such things as having a physical examination or other details, she kept plaguing my brother with them. My brother had once made a trip to the West on company business and so knew quite well what to take and what not to take. Since he was quite busy, though, I didn't want to bother him too much, but whenever my mother begged him to look after something he always shrugged his shoulders and did what he could. My sister-in-law also looked after various things, especially the buying. As for me, my expression always seemed to say, "Who's going anywhere anyhow?" and I spent as much time as possible with Natsuko.

Nevertheless, I couldn't keep my face free of concern forever. Ordering clothes, buying shoes and hats, taking the necessary pictures required my physical presence. There was also the obligation to make calls on various persons. I wasted my time on all sorts of trifling business. Furthermore, even though my uncle was taking care of most of my expenses, I felt that the more money I had the better. So I had my friends sell my

manuscripts for me and I was writing twice as much as usual
to keep them supplied. Naturally, all this tired me. Consequently, I was eager to put my mind to rest by going somewhere
with Natsuko where we would be completely alone. The place
I chose was a hotel I had been to once before.

On the tacit assumption that after my return I would be
spending every day with her in this fashion, I put aside all
restraint and acted as if I felt that I was already half her
husband. But Natsuko refused to let me go any farther than
to kiss her.

"After you come back," Natsuko insisted when things became
dangerous. I did not want to insist on more than that. I was
satisfied to postpone my happiness until I got back.

"I was afraid you would do a somersault at the party the
other day."

"I don't give myself as easily as all that. Not any more!
There's only one person now I'd put on such a silly show for."

"A very fortunate chap, I'd say!"

"I want to make him more and more fortunate."

"On behalf of that person, I thank you."

"I don't like to have you say 'on behalf of'!"

"In that case, let me say that when I get back I shall thank
you on my own behalf."

"If only I could make the next half year go faster!"

"If only we could! I'm going only because it will multiply
the joy of our being together again a hundred times."

"You said at the party that you're going only for the pleasure
of returning. I'm sure only one person present understood what
you really meant."

"That person I offer my life."

"If you say that, you may be punished by the gods. They
are said to be very jealous," said Natsuko playfully.

"I think I'm the happiest person in the whole world!"

"You're only the second."

"Who's first, then?"

"You don't know? You're awfully stupid."

"You're the one who's second, or maybe not even that."

"Oh no! I'm first!"

This innocent argument was somehow very delightful.

I must confess that my thoughts were not completely innocent. I did not lack erotic desire, but I couldn't bring myself to ask her to do a handstand in her kimono. Her purity made me want to keep myself pure likewise. I resolved to save all such pleasure for the day of our marriage after my return.

We played Japanese chess and ping pong. I won at chess but was completely outclassed at ping pong. I take pride in my game, but she was in another class altogether.

Time passed all too quickly. There were things I had wanted to talk over with her, but in her presence I forgot all about them. Nevertheless, with things still left to do before my departure the next day, I could not be too utterly relaxed. I had promised to have dinner at home with my mother, brother, and sister-in-law, so we had to leave the hotel at three.

"Please write to me, won't you?"

"You too."

"Of course I will. But you mustn't make fun of my writing."

"I promise. We'll both be a lot maturer when we meet again."

"Are you hinting that I'm a little scattered-brained now?"

"You *are* if it gives you any pleasure to make such innuendos!"

"Oh you're not so wise either if you take much pride in seeing through me!"

"Let's call it a draw!"

"Okay. I mean it now, please hurry back."

"I will. Remember, I'm going only for the pleasure of coming back."

"My one joy will be to see the days pass."

"Once I'm aboard ship the passing of the days will be my greatest joy too."

"You'll make yourself awfully unpopular there."

"I'll try hard to square myself."

"Please take care of your health. I'm so healthy it's disgusting. My brother once remarked, 'You never seem to realize it when you're sick. By the time you do, you're well again.' "

"Your body isn't yours alone any more."

"You too please keep in mind that your body isn't yours alone."

I couldn't help marveling that two people should be granted such happiness—a happiness from which lovely children would be born and later grandchildren. I had the feeling that somewhere someone was showering blessings on us and I was grateful. Poor groping humanity!

19

I reached home in high spirits. Everybody was there waiting for me. They seemed surprised at my light-heartedness.

"Where have you been?" asked my brother.

"With a friend," I said evasively.

My mother said, "The day is here at last!"

It was to be a simple dinner, but it was more sumptuous than usual. To my surprise the saké cups were brought out and my mother filled my cup with our best ceremonial saké. If only Natsuko were here, I said to myself.

After the meal was finished, I asked my brother if I could have a talk with him. "About what?" he said as he followed me out of the room.

"Do you know Nonomura-san, Sir?" I asked, coming right to the point.

"Of course I know him!"

"I'm thinking of marrying Nonomura's younger sister when I get back," I said. Taken aback a bit, my brother thought a moment.

"It would be better to decide on that after you get back."

"I thought I'd better let you know what I have in mind."

"I understand. I believe the girl's all right."

"Do you know her?"

"Yes I do."

"Thank you!" I said earnestly. My brother made no reply.

"Does Mother know?"

"She was fretting somewhat about it. But it'll be all right to tell her everything now. She said to me the other day, 'If you think she's all right, I won't object.' "

"Is that really true?"

"It's true."

I was so happy, I could have wept. How delighted Natsuko would be to hear this, I thought to myself. I had a sudden urge to tell Natsuko.

"I'm going out for a moment."

"Where to?"

"Nonomura's house."

"Ha, ha, ha! So that's it! Better not get back too late. You've got to think of Mother's feelings too."

"Of course. I'll be right back!" I cried, dashing out of the house.

20

When I arrived at Nonomura's in great haste, Nonomura fortunately was out. Natsuko came flying to meet me.

"Has anything unusual happened?"

"Nothing especially unusual."

"I was a little frightened, thinking something unexpected had come up."

"Did you think I had given up the trip?"

"Would that you had!" she said laughing. "But I really didn't think that," she added. "I was worried. You had gone home far too late."

"There's nothing to worry about. I just wanted to see you right now," I said, stepping ahead of her into her own room.

"And I you. I was a bit restless and had just finished putting my room in order when I realized that you were back. I thought I was dreaming. Then I wondered if something had happened."

Natsuko's room was in perfect order. I was startled to see a picture of myself taken by Nonomura in a beautiful frame on her desk. Of course I was delighted, but seeing it made me want to have one of Natsuko too. She had already given me one to carry with me, but I wanted many more.

"Please show me all the pictures you have of yourself," I begged.

"Is that what you came here for—to snatch pictures?" said Natsuko laughing.

"That's not at all why I came. It's really nothing important—only that I just told my brother about my plan to marry you after I get back."

"You did?"

"My brother said he knows you and that it would be all right. I learned from him that my mother knew about us and was secretly pleased."

"Really?"

"Then I got permission from my brother to see you right away."

Natsuko took my hand and looked at me smiling. Her eyes were bright with tears.

A tumult of thoughts passed through my mind and tears came to my eyes.

"A truly wonderful person, your brother, isn't he? I'm delighted with your mother too."

"You'll make a good daughter for my mother and a fine sister for my brother."

"Oh yes. I intend to be. But I want especially to be a good wife to you."

Natsuko looked especially tender and sweet just then.

"Please bring your pictures."

"All right!" she said, hurrying to get them from her dresser.

Among them were pictures taken when she was a baby. They were all lovely. Those of her at eight, twelve, fourteen, and seventeen were equally lovely. The most recent ones suffered from comparison with the flesh and blood object, but I selected several of the latest.

"I'll take these."

"Greedy!" she said laughing.

"Miserly!" I retorted.

"Don't be so snippy or there'll be a fight."

"When a fellow's challenged to a fight, he can't back down."

We both took boxing stances, giving way to peals of laughter. But after the laughter had died away, we felt a strange hollowness. I wanted to stay forever. But I remembered my mother waiting patiently for me.

"I think I'd better go home now, don't you?"

"Go home? Isn't your home wherever I am?"

"In that case, may I step out now?"

"Your mother is probably waiting for you, so please go."

"Well, I'll just step out for a bit then."

"Run along now."

But I didn't get up from my cushion. Suddenly we threw ourselves into each other's arms and kissed. Then we got up and went out together. As we approached my house we made a wide circle around it.

When I got back to my family about an hour had passed. My mother smiled as she welcomed me. My brother smiled too.

21

The next day I finally left Tokyo. I was to take my boat from Kobe. At my mother's urging, my brother insisted on accompanying me to Kobe. My mother could not bring herself to go farther than the front door of the house. It made me sad, of course, to part from my mother.

Twenty or thirty persons had come to see me off at the Tokyo Station. Natsuko was there, of course. She was with Nonomura. Nonomura came up to me. "I learned that you came to my house last night," he said in a low voice. "I'm sorry I was out. My sister said it was better that way though." Then he added, "I'll make myself responsible for her while you're away, so go with an easy heart."

"I'll be so grateful if you do."

Natsuko was listening to our conversation with obvious joy. She was wearing kimono and was more demure than usual. I introduced them both to my brother. He greeted them simply but not coldly.

"Thank you for your many kindnesses to my brother," he said. "My mother is quite happy about the whole thing."

"I am too, I assure you!" said Nonomura. Natsuko made a polite bow without saying anything. Her modesty was so touching that I pretended to be amused and looked at her and smiled. Natsuko, noticing my manner, looked up and smiled back.

People kept coming up now one after another to greet me. In the constant flow of persons there were intervals like the ebbing of the sea. During one of them Natsuko suddenly darted over to me and said, "I'm so very healthy, so you don't have to worry about me, but please don't fail to come back in six months."

"I won't, you can depend on it. And what a happy day that will be for me!"

Just then some thoughtless persons came crowding around. Natsuko made a curtsey and withdrew.

At last it was time for the train to start. I put my head out of the window and waved to everybody. Natsuko waved her handkerchief. I wanted to keep watching her forever, but my view was soon cut off by the crowds gathered there to see off their friends. Then the train reached a point from which the platform itself was no longer visible. Only then did I return to my seat.

"Nonomura's sister is a wonderful girl, isn't she! If only Mother had been here to meet her!" said my brother with a kindness that warmed my heart.

At Kobe I boarded my ship.

22

I don't care to write much here about my voyage. I might say, however, that despite my loneliness it was quite enjoyable. I was seeing a part of the world I had known nothing about until now. I'm not much good aboard ship, but by lying flat on my back I managed to ward off sea-sickness. The ocean makes one think. When looking out over the sea I always thought of Natsuko. The sight of anything unusual made me regret that Natsuko was not by my side.

It was also interesting to note how completely the customs differed in the various ports at which the ship touched.

At each port I wrote to my mother and to Natsuko, but it goes without saying that the letter to Natsuko was the longer one.

Then a month and a half later I was in Paris. My uncle's house was already crowded with his own children, so I rented a cheap room and came to my uncle's only for meals. But before I describe my daily routine I will mention something about a letter from Natsuko and my answer to it. From them you will get an idea of what my life was like at that time.

I had a Japanese as companion all the way to Paris. When I reached Paris my uncle was there to meet me. He was an employee in a Japanese bank. If my uncle hadn't met me in Paris I believe I would have been very much upset. But that too is something that appears in my letter to Natsuko. Being met by my uncle upon arriving in Paris made me happy enough, but being handed a letter from Natsuko when we reached my uncle's house thrilled me much more. My uncle was already aware that Natsuko was my fiancée. He had been informed by my mother.

With a pounding heart I read Natsuko's letter.

"This has been a truly wonderful day. I have been worrying, but your letter from Shanghai, which I just received, has put my mind at ease. Thank you so much! Your being safe so far on the voyage makes me very happy. There is never an end to things to worry about. I have always been an optimist and not much given to worry, but this time I did worry. After our parting at the Tokyo Station I felt terribly lonely and depressed. I returned home alone and had a good cry. Realizing that this is your great opportunity, I had resolved to keep back my tears, but my tears would not heed my resolution and gushed out and I felt wretched. But after crying a while I felt better again. Couldn't I still get to Kobe in time to see you once more, I asked myself in anguish. Oh, why hadn't I gone with you to Kobe! As long as I knew you were still in Japan it was hard to resign myself. When I realized today that you had definitely left Shimonoseki behind you, I became calmer. There was no longer anything I could do. At Tokyo Station you seemed strangely lost too. Until then I had not realized that separation could be such a painful thing. But how much more happy your return will be because of it. The thought thrills me even now. My constant prayer is that time will pass quickly.

"Your situation is a little better than mine. You're seeing all sorts of things and having all sorts of new experiences and that makes me envious. But I am a Japanese woman. I am your wife. I mustn't spend all my time complaining. My brother is relieved because I seem in better spirits than he expected. What I feel inside he doesn't know. I don't want him to know. It's enough that a certain person knows. My dearest dearest one. The one staring at me from my desk.

"I'm thinking of starting my koto lessons again. Since you seem to like my playing the koto, I'm going to get so good at it by the time you get back that you will be amazed. And I've also finally gotten around to learning to cook. And when my mother told me I was to study sewing too, I was delighted. It's amazing how I've changed. I want to be a really worth-while person by the time you get back. But I'll probably do a lot of nagging too. If you carry on like my brother does I will be a nagger.

"Sometimes I'm very depressed and sometimes very happy. When I realize that you will be reading this letter in Paris, I get a strange feeling. I believe it will reach Paris before you and will be awaiting you. Paris—what sort of place is it? I suppose you'll lose no time getting to the Louvre. If only I were with you! But I'll be patient and wait for you to come back. I keep toying with the idea of getting my brother to go to Paris. But he is awfully busy and probably won't like the idea. My brother is the one who should have gone. It was wicked of him to get you to go when he himself would not. But it's only because of his great hopes for you that he urged you to go, so I shouldn't be angry with him.

"I keep talking about nothing but you, and my brother says he's getting tired of it, but I won't let up. He acts as if his annoying little sister is an affliction. Well, it serves him right. If he hadn't got you to go I would be seeing you every day and wouldn't be feeling so lonely and worried. I'm always wondering whether you are in good health, but I have no way of finding out. But you must have arrived safely to be reading this letter, so I congratulate you with all my heart. No matter how wonderful a place Paris is, don't forget to come back. Please don't delay a single day.

"My brother said to me rather mournfully this morning, 'Poor Muraoka! To think he will be under the thumb of a wife like you!'

" 'Muraoka is not the sort of person one has to keep under thumb. He is quite different from you,' I was replying heatedly when I realized to my horror that my sister-in-law was standing near by.

"I'm afraid I'm too sharp-tongued. I feel I have often said very rude things, but knowing that you understand me, I don't worry.

"Now please take very very good care of yourself.

"I am as healthy as ever. At times I'm disgusted at my good health. I have felt that it might be nice to be just a little sick so that people would pity me, but now I want to keep getting healthier and healthier. I exercise regularly. I'm counting the days before you return on my fingers. I've put circles around one hundred and thirty days and every day I cross out one with a real feeling of excitement. First thing after I get up in the morning, I cross off a circle. If only I could cross off a hundred at a stroke.

"The person who said that the months and days fly past is a great liar, I am thinking resentfully just now.

"Yesterday I took a stroll past your house. Nothing seemed amiss there, so I returned home with my mind at ease. But I had a strong desire to see your mother. Everything awaits your return.

"There are so many things I want to write, but I don't know where to begin. The next letter will be more to the point. Take better and better care of yourself, I beg you. Your body is not yours alone, say I preaching to Buddha. I am waiting for your letter."

My aunt and uncle and cousins gave me even a more friendly reception than I had expected. My uncle, visibly elated, said that he had never believed that he would see me in Paris.

Claiming tiredness, I withdrew to the room set aside for me and immediately wrote a letter to Natsuko.

"I am in Paris at last. The best thing about getting here was finding a letter from you. (I'm using the familiar form of *you* deliberately. In my reveries about you on the ship I formed the habit of talking to you in intimate language.) On arrival at Paris this evening, I was met by my uncle and taken by taxi directly to his house—it would be more correct to say rooms. My uncle has rented four. They're not first-class, but they're well arranged.

"I can't say that I have seen Paris yet. I will write again after I have had a look at Paris, but I saw nothing wrong in writing before. I am scheduled to go to the Louvre with my cousin tomorrow. He is twenty-two and is interested in painting himself. He is a fine, sensitive young man and he seems to like me. My uncle knows that I can stay only three months at the most, but he tried to persuade me to stay longer. My aunt, however, said, 'But there is someone waiting for him.'

" 'I once thought my sister was worried about that, but she is apparently happy about it now, so everything must be all right,' said my uncle smiling at my aunt.

"Our relationship is now a public matter and everyone is congratulating me. From that point of view there are no two persons as fortunate as we. It's because wherever you are known your praises are sung. Our brother's fine reputation also has something to do with it. It feels strange to call him 'our brother' but I just had the urge to try writing it. Why I should be so kindly treated by everybody and so blessed by fate is beyond me. I've got to be exemplary from now on, I realize.

"That you're making yourself a good wife for me delights me, but I want you to become a more and more cheerful wife. For you to be overly docile is contrary to your nature. I want you to be more cheerful and lively. Since I am rather introspective myself, a cheerful, serene, unworried wife by my side would be a great help. In that respect also you are ideal. I'm glad to see you improving your performance on the koto, but you must not neglect to become more expert in the handstand too. You needn't be afraid that I will try to make money from your talent.

"The voyage was blessed with remarkably fine weather. A chap who had made the trip three times said that it was the first time he had experienced such a smooth sailing. 'That's because someone's praying for us,' I wanted to say, but I didn't. I would probably have been considered a bit touched if I had. It makes me smile. I'm awfully happy! I've already picked the ship to take me back. I should be arriving at Kobe one hundred and forty-three days from today. If the ship is on time, I should be in Kobe on November 12th!! The ship is the M Maru. By the time you get this letter there will be only about one hundred and thirty days left. When I think that there are still more than a hundred days to go, I am somewhat depressed. But then when I think of what awaits me after that, I realize that I mustn't ask for everything.

"By this time you should have received the card I sent you from Naples. I admired the scenery of Naples and the art museums. The excavations of Pompeii were more splendid than I had imagined. I found it interesting to speculate how it must have looked in its heyday. Everywhere there were places I would have enjoyed strolling along with a certain person.

"Oh, the magnificence of the scenery visible from the train from Marseilles! The brightness of the landscapes so suggestive of Cezanne or Van Gogh!! I felt I had never seen anything to equal them even in my dreams. I had the feeling that I understood now that Cezanne and Van Gogh had not so much painted a vision of beauty as merely reproduced what they saw.

"As I went farther and farther north, the colors became more and more subdued. I kept staring at the French countryside everywhere dotted with cows and horses, never once turning away from the window all the way to Paris. I was fortunate enough to have a Japanese companion all the way, so I got there without any trouble. I kept thinking how nice it would be for the both of us to come here some day after I had made enough money. By that time there would be youngsters to keep us company. Four or five of them resembling you and me— or is four or five too many? Please don't think badly of me for having such dreams, my sweetest girl! My eternal goddess! Poor taste this, you think? But you really are a sacred thing to me. I realize that you are a woman of flesh and blood, but God has sent you to me as his own special gift. I can't believe otherwise. Perhaps I am speaking too frankly. But it's really delightful to imagine the two of us some years from now coming to Paris accompanied by our children. I indulge myself in silly dreams of our having children of seventeen or eighteen then while we ourselves are only thirty-five or thirty-six.

"The passing of the days is my greatest pleasure too. I'm going to follow your example and draw one hundred and forty-three circles right now and then, beginning tomorrow, cross out one each day.

"I have looked at your picture hundreds of times. I intend to show it to my aunt and uncle tomorrow. I wanted to show it before this, but I couldn't quite bring myself to do it. It's something to be proud of. Whenever I look at your picture I imagine myself seeing that inexpressibly charming and coquettish look you gave me when you cried, 'Greedy!'

"Sleep well, my darling, darling Natsuko. I wonder what time it is now in Tokyo. It's eleven in the evening here. It must be morning in Tokyo. I suppose I ought to say, 'Good morning!' Time for you to cross out another circle and do your exercises. Or is it already time for you to be having breakfast?

"I am excited at the thought of going to the Louvre tomorrow. Well, I'm going to say, 'Good night!' anyhow.

"Remember . . . the 12th of November!!

"My dear, dear Natsuko!"

23

By the time I received an answer to this letter mailed from Paris, there were five others from Natsuko. But I won't bother to copy out all of them. As examples of our correspondence I will present the answer to my Paris letter, the last of the five, and my reply to it.

"Your letter from Paris is here at last! How I waited for it! You must have seen Paris by now. And within twenty days at most your letter about it ought to be here . . . It really ought to get here much sooner . . . These are the thoughts going through my mind these past three or four days which I have spent mostly in going back and forth to the mail box. Time after time I am disappointed. But no matter how many times I am disappointed, I always go right back trembling with excitement for another look.

"From now on I don't think I will be quite so impatient. The day your letter came I was so excited that my sarcastic, lynx-eyed brother took one look at my face and said, 'Got your letter, eh? What does it say?' He had hit it right on the head, so I must admit he's no fool. At such times I always get back at him by making him more jealous. I don't quit until he runs off saying, 'Stop it! Stop it!' On the other hand, when I don't get a letter for a week my disposition is bad and everybody treats me very carefully.

"Sometimes my brother—whether to cheer me up or to vent his irritation, I'm not sure—will say, 'It can't possibly be here yet.'

" 'I know that,' I say.

" 'If you know it, what's the point of going to the mail box again and again? The ship is getting farther and farther away. It now takes twice as long for a letter to get here.'

" 'I know that!'

" 'And knowing that, you go to the mail box anyhow?'

" 'I feel like having a look and so I do.'

" 'That's why I say your thinking is not scientific enough.'

" 'You, Sir, are much too scientific in your thinking. I detest such people!'

"This is the sort of silly talk I'm capable of when I'm irritated. With my brother annoyed at my foolishness, I fire a second shot.

" 'Sir, you don't understand human emotions very well, do you? How do you expect to write good novels?'

"Then my brother replies, 'I'm going to write one about our little Natsuko entitled, "The Silly Goose".'

" 'Go ahead and write one, if you can! I won't read it though.'

"Then in a pout, I go to the mail box for another look. I'm in hopes that by some miracle a letter from you will be there, but there isn't any after all. Then, pretending unconcern, as if returning from a walk, I go into my own room when my brother isn't looking, lock it from inside, and enter a certain person's world.

"Then, in front of your picture, I play the koto, do my exercises, and do various other things that I can't talk about yet. When my brother has left, I go down and take another look at the mail box. I feel a bit embarrassed in front of the mail box. But the mail box does not say sarcastic things as my brother does. It's always rather indifferent.

"Today I'm really in excellent spirits. My brother caught me in the act of returning from a look at the mail box. From my lack-luster manner, he guessed that no letter had come, but because I looked so very dejected, he said nothing. I was in my room, lost in thought, when my sister-in-law entered.

" 'Won't you have some tea, Natsuko-san?' she said.

" 'Thank you, I will,' I replied cheerfully. Anything at all to make the time go faster is all right with me. So I went and had tea with my brother and his family. Then I had an urge again to go to the mail box. When I got up suddenly, my brother guessed my intention at once and said, laughing, 'You've just come from there, and now you want to go again?'

"Without replying, I went out. When I got to the mail box, sure enough, there were three letters for my brother and also yours from Paris. I deliberately put on a dejected look and with the words, 'Nothing much,' handed my brother his letters.

"My brother, wanting to console me said kindly, 'Even your Muraoka would have too much to do on reaching Paris to write at once.'

" 'Really?' I said with a quizzical look. Then I calmly drew your letter from the folds of my kimono and opened the envelope.

" 'What, it's come?'

" 'He wouldn't be able to write at once, you say?' I said, starting to read the letter. Then, overcome by the realization that you had written without a moment's delay, I flew into my own room. Safely inside, I danced round and round. 'Wonderful! Wonderful!' my heart kept saying. I was able to cross out six circles in one stroke and my heart was singing.

"The 12th of November! I will, of course, come dashing to Kobe. I was so happy I couldn't hold back the tears. I ran to my brother's quarters and blurted out excitedly that you were arriving in Kobe the 12th of November.

"My brother looked at me blankly. 'Isn't that still a bit far off?' he said.

"Never before in my life had I considered him so stupid. My sister-in-law was more understanding. 'The 12th of November!' she exclaimed. 'How wonderful! It'll be here in no time!' You can see why I'm so fond of my sister-in-law.

"My life now has something to point to. The 12th of November—won't that be a wonderful day? I will direct all my thought and action toward that day. Please, please, take care of your health and I will take better care of mine. The food and the climate there are different from ours, so please be more and more careful!

"Please give my regards to your aunt and uncle and, by all means, let them see my picture. This very minute my likeness is moving through Paris attached to you! Yes, it certainly will be a wonderful day when I can come to Paris with you accompanied by our children. I would be happy going anywhere at all with you.

"I intend never to lose my good spirits again. Until now I haven't been able to help myself, though, because a thief had stolen my good spirits along with my heart and had run off with them to Paris. But today a part of them has come back. Oh glorious 12th of November! I am waiting, waiting for your coming!

"Oh, that meeting in Kobe! I'll be all in tears! And happy! My dearest, dearest you. Your faithful one."

24

"I have just returned from my excursion and have been made very happy by your letter. I sent you a number of letters and cards along the way which you must have received by now. I'm convinced now that taking this trip was a good thing. I'm sure I've gained a good deal. Just how much I've gained though, I probably won't know until after I'm back in Japan.

"The very first thing on the program after I get back is setting up a home for you and me. With my limited funds I am buying nothing on my excursions except decorations for our home or such useful practical items as you would heartily approve of. Such shopping has been one of my greatest pleasures on this voyage. Sometimes I think I have gone abroad expressly to buy things for a blissful home with you. Quite an amusing thought. I didn't realize until now that I'm such a sentimentalist. Never had occasion to find out. I'm glad to know that I am. Life is happy and vibrant with hope!

"Wherever one goes one sees only Occidentals. My cousin always accompanies me and he has made things easy, but somehow I have the feeling that we are looked down upon. At such times, however, I remind myself that I have a wonderful country, a home to return to, and someone to love, and that that someone is waiting for me. Then filled with pride, I chide the Westerners inwardly, 'There is a joy waiting for me in that distant land of mine which you can never taste.' Can anyone match me in the splendor of my spiritual possessions? A solitary Japanese among a group of Occidentals is hardly an imposing figure. This is due to a large extent to our not being suited to Western style clothes, but even if we try to make something of the color of our skin and our physique, we still have very little to boast about. Nevertheless, I am confident that from the standpoint of spiritual power and intelligence we are not in the least inferior. The majority of Europeans love pleasure too much. Few of them have any faith in a future life. For the most part they live idly from day to day. Whether it's because they are too much aware of the difficulties of getting money, of the benefits that money brings, or of the misery of not having money, they seem to view everything from the standpoint of money. But it may be that I feel this so keenly because I'm only a traveller among them.

"I want to become an increasingly stronger person and I have the urge to make myself superior to them in spiritual power.

"They are for the most part satisfied with their own culture. They show by their expression that they feel no need to be interested in anything beyond it. Among them there are, of course, many prepossessing and strikingly handsome persons. But not one of them sees any merit in me. That is natural enough, though, and I'm not especially looking for one who will.

"There is one person who does understand me—a certain Japanese girl. She will suffice. When this thought has filled my heart, I walk through their crowded places with a calm spirit and without the slightest feeling of envy.

"I have no talent for foreign languages. Therefore I can't converse with these people, and when I go to a play I observe their laughter and excitement with a blank look. But, fortunately, there are music and painting. They are a world language. I being a lover of art and my cousin a painter, we take great pleasure in looking at the masterpieces. They are the only things I envy them for.

"What splendid works of the Egyptian, Grecian, Renaissance, and other periods are on display here! But when I look at them I also think of the Kannon figures in our Dream Palace or the Kudera Kannon at Nara. No work here compares with them in depth of meaning.

" 'Got you there!' I say to myself. But I can't help wishing that we had a Venus of Milo in Japan.

"I believe it was right for me to come. I believe, too, that coming here has made me appreciate your worth more than ever. I feel that I'm much luckier than I deserve.

"Today is the 20th of August and there are only eighty-four circles left to cross out. A month from now I plan to leave Paris and see Italy with my cousin. I think you had better send your reply to this letter to Naples in care of the NYK Line.

"The days are passing. The circles are being crossed out one by one. I often wish I could fly back. It's a bit far for that. I mustn't ask for the impossible. After all, we will see plenty of each other later. Once I'm back I will never leave you again for a single day. Our life of happiness begins then. But I'm afraid that we might be punished if we are too hedonistic. I hope that our life together will be harmonious, dedicated to hard work, duty, and serious thought. But when I think of how happy our home will be under your management,

I can't help smiling. This is the happiest time of life! We are very fortunate to be able to have such happy dreams. With gratitude to the God I cannot see, I shall try to wait patiently for that joyous day.

"May he pour blessings over two persons yearning for the 12th of November.

"Some day you and I will walk the streets of Paris together. I always go walking with my cousin, taking in the sights without learning the names of the streets, the gardens, or the cathedrals, but I see many places I am eager to show you. Few of our people who have lived in Paris for some time want to return to Japan. But I can't help myself! I've got to go—got to be back! If you know the answer why, raise your hand.

"My dearest, dearest Natsuko."

25

Although I myself did not feel that time was passing fast enough, it was quietly moving on. The days left for me to spend in Paris were getting fewer and fewer. I mailed Natsuko a picture-postcard almost every day. From Natsuko, in turn, came a letter every third day or so. We were both waiting with singleness of heart for the days to pass.

As the time for me to leave Paris approached, I spent more and more time sight-seeing and shopping. I myself could afford to buy only a few inexpensive things, but my uncle, wanting to give Natsuko a present but not knowing what would please her, gave me a one-thousand-franc bill instead. With that I bought her a wrist watch. It was not an elegant one, but it looked much better than we deserved. On the back of it I had engraved the initials N. M., which indicated that the watch was the property of Natsuko Muraoka.

The day for me to leave Paris finally arrived. My aunt and uncle looked sad at the prospect of my leaving. At the same time they were delighted at the thought of my having a family of my own.

I left Paris for Italy on September 15 accompanied by my cousin and we stopped to do sight-seeing at Milan, Florence, and Rome. I wanted to spend as much time as possible in Florence and Rome. My cousin was delighted. Carried away by all the wonderful things to see, I actually forgot to think about time.

What made me happiest of all was the realization that although I was not thinking about the passing of time, the day of my arrival in Japan and my meeting Natsuko was approaching.

Fortunately, I did not have a single day's illness the whole time. I sent Natsuko picture-postcards and letters from various points along the way. In four or five days I was to sail from Naples. I was eager to get to Naples quickly. Since my cousin, bless him, wanted to do some painting in Naples, we pressed on to Naples a bit ahead of schedule.

When I visited the mail ship, Natsuko's letter, as I had hoped, was there. I read it excitedly.

"I realize that this is the last letter I can send to the place at which you are ending your journey, and I am overcome by a rush of feeling. I can imagine how wonderful your travels have been. The next time I shall certainly go along. I'm tired of keeping the home-fires burning. No matter how hard I try to be cheerful, I have strange attacks of loneliness. Every day I pray that you will be oh so very very safe on your journey.

"I suppose you will be boarding your ship right after reading this. If that is the case, then every second the ship is bringing my darling one closer to me. A truly precious ship!—A treasure ship!

"You say you're bringing lots of presents—how wonderful! When I open them I'll be so thrilled I'll think I'm in a dream and will scream with joy and I don't expect to be able to keep myself from turning at least three somersaults. I can't wait to see the watch for Natsuko Muraoka. Today is September 12. Just two more months! It'll be a long two months, but November 12 is bound to come.

"My brother will come to Kobe too. The other day something very delightful happened. Your dear brother very kindly sent my brother and me some tickets for a play. O course, I eagerly accepted his invitation. And do you know whom I met there—it's a great honor for me to be able to tell you this. . . . Have you guessed? Our Mother! I call her Mother too now. She's such a sweet gentle person. I was so excited, I completely lost track of what was happening in the play.

"You're the one who put your brother up to this, I'm told. A praiseworthy act, Sir! I now live only for your return!

"I don't like weak-spirited women, so I'm going to force myself to be cheerful and to endure until you get back. I get so much pleasure from reading your letters and cards. I'm really determined to save money so that I can go travelling with you some day.

"Every morning I get up at six, make the beds, and do all the housework alone without the help of a maid. I'm trying now to live each day with the same attitude of mind as if I were already living with you. Isn't that admirable? After getting up, I wash my face, fix my hair, put on my clothes, and then quickly greet a certain person; then I take my exercises, and, after a short rest, I eat breakfast. In spite of everything, it tastes so delicious, so I take four helpings. Since I'm not the proverbial guest who's over-stayed her welcome, I feel that I can eat a fourth helping without qualms. After that I read a bit from a certain person's books. Then I try reading some

of his poetry in a low voice. Then I do some sewing. If you
guess what I'm sewing, I'll give you a prize. My sewing teacher,
teasingly, suggested that I start on baby clothes. Might come
in handy some day, she said. So I made two children's kimonos—
one for a boy, the other for a girl. I hope to have use for them
some day. They're lying tucked away in my dresser drawer.
Now that I've completed them, I'm sewing a summer robe for
a certain some one. I never cared for sewing much but now
it has suddenly become a delightful pastime because I keep
thinking of a certain person while doing it. My teacher is a
rather wise old bird, don't you think?

"Then there's the koto teacher calling on me three times a
week. I've just been flattered as being very good. I'm much
better than I was in that silly skit. You must be dying to hear
me. I'm going to make you listen even if you refuse. I've come
to believe of late that I have finally learned to express feeling
in my music. It's simply a question of putting yourself into it,
I'm convinced. My brother, hearing me play, said there was
something seductive about it, and I gave him a push. I'd like
to give you a push too, because when you read this, you will
certainly be thinking things which will deserve a push. I'm a
mind-reader and I know you. Have I guessed right? If I have
really hit the mark, I'm delighted.

"And I'm learning to cook too. I make it a point to learn
only practical, inexpensive dishes. I'm already quite good at it.
If you don't hurry back, I won't serve you any of my rare
dishes. My mother and sister-in-law are sometimes disturbed
at my strange concoctions. If you think you're going to be
clever and delay a bit in coming back until I've improved, I've
got something up my sleeve too. I'll get to be a real expert
at making rare dishes and surprise you. It'll serve you right if I
become one before you get here.

"Dear November 12th, please hurry! Don't you think it pathetic for a poor creature to be yearning for you as if each day were a thousand years.

"Every last thing has been done. Now only your return is needed.

"I'm worried about your saying that you're thinner. If you should get sick now, I'll be terribly miserable. I'm annoyed at myself for having become such a silly goose.

"You're reading this letter in Naples, I suppose. Soon you'll be aboard ship. So the day for your return has finally come. As before, I will pray every day that you are safe and that the ship is on time. If the sea is calm, please credit it to my prayers. If the waves are high, please attribute it to my passion—no that's a lie! I will pray every day that your voyage is a good one.

"From your faithful one yearning for that happy happy day. Here's to November 12th at Kobe!"

26

I am not a god. I had no idea what the future held in store for me. What supreme happiness reading Natsuko's letter gave me! Knowing that if I sent a letter by way of Siberia, it would arrive four or five days earlier than if it went by ship, I sat down joyfully to write.

"At Naples at last, and I've just read your letter! Banzai! Three days more and I'll be on the ship leaving Naples.

"Sayonara Europe! I hope to be back some day. I won't be alone then. My darling will be with me. I won't feel the loneliness then that I feel now and I will see your finest treasures to my heart's content.

"I am a man from the East singing the praises of your peoples. But it is as a mountain saluting a mountain, not as a slave bowing before his master. Just as we recognize your worth, you must recognize the worth of the East. I have been astounded at the beauty of your Greek sculptures. If I brought one of them to the center of Tokyo, how the people would marvel at it! Your exquisite marbles—I can't conceive how the human form could be portrayed more beautifully!

"And yet, the more I observe of Greek sculpture, the more I bow to our Kannons at Yumedono and Kudera. Each type evokes a completely different response. I won't try to say which is the more satisfying.

"But I can't say that I admire the Greek the more. The Oriental has its mysticism, its spiritual grandeur, its expression of infinite benevolence. Nevertheless, I must concede that there is no beauty like that of Greece in the Orient. It is good to have both! We mustn't be without either!

"I have seen Leonardo da Vinci. I have seen Michaelangelo. I have seen Raphael. I have seen Titian and Rembrandt. I have seen the splendid murals of Fra Angelico. It's a pity I couldn't see those of Giotto, but I surely will next time.

"But in the East we have Kirumin. We have Ryokai. We have Bokkai. We have Kukai, Tobano Sojo, Mitsuhaga, Nobuzone, Sesshu, and many many others. Think of all the Buddhistic statuary!

"As an Oriental I don't feel that I have to lower my eyes one bit, and I don't feel that I have met anyone with more spiritual power than I. I don't understand the language of the people here, but communication between minds can be carried on through the eyes and facial expressions. Any spiritual greatness would have been communicated to me directly through their involuntary actions. I know there is something in the Europeans which keeps them from being inferior to us, but I

have felt intuitively that we are not in the least inferior to them.
I am happy to have acquired the understanding that Nonomura
expected me to acquire and I commend his keen insight.

"In my excitement I've rambled awfully. But you will
certainly understand and pardon my wanting to pour myself
out on the eve of my departure from Europe.

"As an Oriental traveling around in Europe I have had to
endure a great deal.

"It's because of the way things are between the East and the
West. I believe that we Orientals still have much to learn from
the West.

"But I feel also that there are a great many things about the
East that we should try to teach the West.

"I would like to take from them what there is to take of
spiritual good and give them what we have to give.

"Feeling as I do, I have never forgot my manners or lost my
good will toward them, but I have seen no special reason for
flattering them. But what a lot of silly tensions I will be relieved of when I get back to Japan! Being aware always that
one is a foreigner among foreigners wherever one goes doesn't
make for peace of mind.

"Four or five days after you read this letter I will reach
Kobe. The joy of that day! A most wonderful gift for the
start of a new life! Let's drink it to the last drop! To deserve
this gift we mustn't forget to be humble. To do good work
and to raise five children—those are our primary obligations.
Materially, an austere life, but spiritually, a life overflowing
with happiness. Always working at my side will be you. As
relaxation from my work, I will have your koto to listen to.
After the day's work, there will be a pleasant walk. Exotic
dishes may be hard to manage, but we won't mind. We will
live in a world of happy dreams. I can't wait to get back.
Everything stands in abeyance until then. Not until then will

the value of this journey be manifest. My dearest dearest
Natsuko. Here's to November 12th at Kobe! When you read
this letter it should already be November."

With my cousin to see me off, I boarded my ship safely on
sailing day. The ship left Naples on schedule.

Europe, adieu! my heart sang. I will certainly come again
some day! Then there will be two of us—or perhaps five or
six, counting the little ones!

Vesuvius was belching smoke. Its outline was beautiful and
inspiring. As I waved to my cousin I also waved sentimentally
to the mountain.

The ship set sail. It turned eastward. From now on every
second was bringing it nearer to Japan. I felt a deep gratitude
to this ship moving so tirelessly ever and ever nearer to Natsuko.
The churning of the screw seemed somehow steady and reassuring. The fact that it was a Japanese ship with Japanese
passengers on board made me doubly happy. Oh wonderful
Japan! One who has never been in a place inhabited only by
Occidentals can never appreciate the joy of returning to you in
one of your ships! Especially someone who speaks only Japanese!

The weather was fine. I felt wonderful in every way. Of
course, I had not forgotten to let my mother and Natsuko know
by wireless that I was safely on board.

I can't say that this trip was unalloyed bliss. At times it
was very hot. But my happiness was not dampened by even
such an annoyance. Time passed all too slowly but there was
no denying that we were heading for Japan. And there, there
was someone waiting! I who ride this ship, my heart kept
singing, am thrilled at the thought of each day bringing me
nearer to you but impatient at the slowness of time. But once
past, this will all be a happy memory.

The joy of a man returning to his native land where
  joy awaits him!
The two who share that joy!
The joy of the one who waits!
The two who share that joy!
Impatient for the twelfth day of the eleventh month!
In Kobe they're to meet—these two.
Ah the joy of it!
May the gods pour blessings over them!
Dearest dearest Natsuko.

27

My greatest concern was that the ship might be late, but
it reached Colombo on schedule and it was also on schedule
at Penang and Singapore. The cabin boy himself reassured me
that with things going as they were we would definitely arrive
in Kobe on November 12th. At Singapore I was startled at
being handed a letter from Natsuko.

"I believed my previous letter would be the last to reach you
on the way. And so when I received the letter with the picture
of you in front of the Notre Dame Cathedral and showed it
joyfully and proudly to my brother, I said, 'It would certainly
be useless to write to him now.'

"But he replied, 'Why not send him a letter by way of
Singapore. It would probably reach him all right. He's very
likely bored with travel and will welcome a letter from you no
matter how long and dull. Write him one so long that he will
have read it only three times by the time he gets to Hongkong
and he will be delighted.'

"Even though he sounded awfully sarcastic, I thought him
rather clever and myself, on the contrary, a bit dense. But I'm

not really a complete fool, so I won't be too severe with myself. The fact is, I'm quite satisfied with things as they are.

"That's why I'm writing so carelessly today—as if determined to bore you to death. Very likely November will have begun by the time you get to read this. So you've reached Singapore at last! Congratulations. Be patient a little longer. No matter how much you suffer you're still breathing. I'm always right with you. It's wonderful that you've been in such fine health. Seeing your picture made me ever so much more eager to be with you. After showing it at least once to everybody, I put it in a frame and hung it on the wall of my room. It was my brother's best frame—one from which I had removed a miniature Leonardo da Vinci. My brother balked at letting me have it, but he finally gave in when I promised that it would be only until November 11. Once you yourself are in Tokyo again there won't be any need for your picture to hang here, will there? The original is after all so much better to have.

"After hanging your picture up, I showed off to you the different things I've learned. Still forty circles left! An awful lot crossed out though!

"Yesterday my mother and brother discussed the wedding ceremony in my presence and suggested that it be simple and informal. Contrary to my usual self, I blushed at the suggestion. When my brother asked, 'Would you prefer it that way?' I said, 'Yes.' Your brother seems to be of the same opinion. My brother apparently meets with him quite often. But I have no idea where.

"And last night I tried to visualize the wedding ceremony. I pictured you with a frown on your face. I had resolved to keep my eyes lowered. But I saw ourselves stealing sidelong glances when no one was looking and smiling at each other. I realized that we were being watched but decided that if we were—well then we were. Then I thought of something funny and laughed to myself.

"I had had the thought that if I should suddenly turn a somersault in front of all these solemn persons, how startled they would be! You would have been delighted, of course, but the others would have considered me out of my mind. But please don't worry—I won't do any such thing. If you tell me to though, of course I will. I mean, if you have the nerve to tell me. . . .

"Then I wondered where we would go afterwards. I had no ideas on the matter. I leave that to you. Enough of that subject now!

"And so I now call myself Natsuko Muraoka.

"I'm writing all this nonsense because I think it must be awfully tiresome on that ship—please keep that in mind as you read.

"Three days ago we had a class reunion party. I attended it so as to make the time go faster.

"There were seventeen girls present and eleven of them were already married. One of them said, 'Are you married?'

" 'No,' I replied.

" 'Are you still a confirmed spinster?' another asked.

" 'I should say not!' I replied coolly. Everybody laughed.

" 'Do you have a sweetheart?' someone asked brazenly. Another, even more brazen, said, 'It's Muraoka-san, isn't it?'

"I couldn't help being embarrassed at this, but I decided to pay them back in kind and said, 'Of course.'

" 'When will you be married?' asked another meddling miss.

" 'That's still a secret,' I said hoping to be let off, but my adversaries were relentless.

" 'I've seen you two,' one of them called out and I couldn't help flinching, but thinking that it would reflect on you if I let myself be vanquished, I said, 'Where?'

" 'So have I !' another teased.

" 'Simply incredible !' still another exclaimed. I was terribly flustered, but I'm ashamed to admit I was really pleased at being teased like this.

" 'You certainly have an ecstatic look about you !' said one of my pursuers, refusing to let up.

" 'You can tease all you want, but you're going to be even more jealous later.'

" 'After you have your own house I'm going to call on you.'

" 'If you can stand the feeling of jealousy, please do.'

" 'Let's all go !' cried one intrepid soul.

" 'It would probably be safer not to !' exclaimed a more cautious one. The clamor became deafening.

"They cheered me up a lot. Come to think of it, I was calmer than any of them, and wasn't that due to a certain person's influence?

"Really, I'm not the person I used to be at all any more.

"I'm getting better and better at the koto. My sensei told me I have a feeling for it. It's undoubtedly sheer flattery, but she says it's a pity I'm remaining an amateur. If I practice a little harder we might be able to make our living expenses from the koto. But I don't think I want to become that good. I play only when I think of a certain person. To be honest, I do it mainly to make the time pass. Once the big day has arrived I will never be bored again. After November 12th the slower the days and months pass the better, but until then I want them to fly swiftly and I'm going to have a conference with Father Time on the matter.

"You are probably bored too on that ship. But you've got a breath left, I'd say. Even if the ship rides a little roughly, I pray that it won't be late. I want you to suffer just a little.

That's a lie. If anyone harms my dearest, dearest one I will turn into a spirit and fight him. Aren't I noble?

"Once you're back I'm sure I'll be a really cheerful woman. I am truly a happy woman. But it's wrong for you to be away. But you *are* coming back, aren't you? It's a solid fact that second after second, minute after minute, hour after hour, day after day the time of your arrival is getting nearer.

"What scares me is the thought that something terrible may happen to you or that you might get sick, and I pray God that you will be spared. I am always dreaming of the meeting in Kobe and the trip back to Tokyo with you. No matter how much we talk I don't think we'll ever get everything said. You're going to find me constantly staring at you, thrusting myself in front of you, showering you with attention. You'll think me a nuisance.

"When I think of the everlasting joy that follows, I'm sure there isn't another creature as lucky as I am.

"I had just finished writing the above when my brother came in and handed me your letter from Milan. So you've finally left Paris! Banzai!

"I read your letter as if in a dream; then I held it in my teeth and turned three somersaults. But this is a secret just between us.

"How is it possible for someone like me to be loved by a man like you? I'm awfully lucky! So you've seen 'The Last Supper.' Is it really so wonderful? I would love to have seen it. It was sweet of you to say that you let my picture see it. But I didn't see a thing myself. Could it be because you're just not saintly enough? Anyhow, you've made me very happy.

"I had just finished the last sentence when my brother yelled out in a raucous voice, 'Natchan, Natchan!'

"I felt like yelling back, 'Shut up!' but I went out instead to see what he wanted. Then I was glad that I had not lost my temper.

"My mother and brother had a letter in front of them and seemed to be having some sort of discussion. It was a letter from your brother to mine saying that after noting the year of my birth and making calculations your mother had discovered that it would be bad luck not to have the wedding this year or at least this year by the old calendar and that she would like to have the wedding no later than next January and she wanted to know how that would suit us.

"My mother and brother both were of the opinion that this was too early and would not leave enough time for preparations, but they felt that since your mother had especially requested it we ought to comply, and they wanted to know what I thought about it.

"I wanted to come right out and say that I certainly had not the least objection to an early wedding, but knowing that the wedding wouldn't be delayed even if I didn't reveal my true feelings, I said merely, 'I have no preference—I leave it all up to you.'

"But my brother, who is never happy unless he is being sarcastic, said, 'You're awfully matter of fact. You should be much more flustered.'

"I was about to give him a sharp answer, but, not wanting to stir up a hornet's nest, I ran off without saying a word.

"I'm going to be your wife eventually. Just now I'm waiting, waiting for you to get here. These days the letters KOBE are always before my eyes. Really now, don't let the ship be late.

"I am a very lucky girl!

"Here's to November 12th at Kobe! Kobe! Kobe!

"My dearest husband!

Your wife."

28

Reading this letter put me beside myself with joy. Soon I would be in Japan. Only 14 or 15 days more!

The ship seemed ready to depart from Singapore, but it didn't sail for some time. Its taking on so much cargo exasperated me. The loading seemed to last forever.

But finally we sailed. How slowly the days dragged! But the ship was definitely making headway. Time was passing. Three days before arrival at Hongkong the sea was as smooth as if oil had been poured over it and a soft breeze was blowing. The purple-bluish water peculiar to the South Seas was strangely beautiful, and in three or four places over the horizon thin gray shrouds, apparently created by squalls, hung from the sky. The forward movement of the ship gave me a pleasant feeling, and the steady hum of the engines proclaiming its soundness was reassuring.

As I stared all alone over the water my thoughts went flying to Japan and I saw myself meeting Natsuko again.

At that moment the cabin boy came and handed me a telegram. I felt that I knew what was inside without opening it: "Awaiting your safe return Natsuko."

It would certainly be something like that even if not those exact words.

So I opened it with a light heart. But the message set down there . . . not being a god, I couldn't possibly have been prepared for it.

"Natsuko passed three a.m. Flu. All deep shock. Sorry. Nonomura."

When I finally translated it into the words, "Natsuko died this morning at three of influenza. We are all deeply shocked. I'm sorry. Nonomura," what grief! what anguish!

Can such a terrible thing really happen to a human being? I asked myself. Convulsed with sobs, I fled to a place where no one could see me and I poured out my heart. But tears, no matter how copious, could not alter what had happened.

It was too, too brutal. Too terrible. How pitiful for Natsuko! I didn't know what to do next. I had an impulse to settle everything by jumping into the ocean.

But at that moment it struck me that some jealous person might be playing a joke on me. Such a possibility could not be rejected.

So I immediately sent the following radiogram to Nonomura: "Received word Natsuko's death. Can't believe it. Is it true?"

Some hours later there was another radiogram.

"Natsuko got sick three days ago and never recovered. Didn't want to let you know but decided you ought to be told first. Poor girl. But she died beautifully and serenely. For your sake was determined not to die, but she did. Oh I have never been so crushed. Nonomura."

29

That human life is a fragile thing subject to all sorts of tragic possibilities I had always understood. But I had never dreamed I would experience this hard truth myself. Did such a splendid, such a wholesome person have to die such a sudden death? That this sweet blossom so breathlessly waiting should at the moment of my coming have been plucked was something my mind simply could not accept.

I looked for a place to be alone but being aboard ship and a second class passenger sharing a cabin, I had no place to cry my heart out.

In the deep of the night when everybody was asleep I wept quietly, muffling my sobs.

But people began to wonder at my appearance. Until now I had constantly been in good spirits. But now I ate very little, kept running off by myself to weep, and, no matter how I tried to hide it, always had swollen red eyes. Some persons realized then that my fiancee had died. I couldn't keep it to myself. Everybody was sympathetic but their sympathy did not touch me very deeply. They began to watch me lest I do something desperate.

I no longer felt that the ship was going too slowly. The thought of reaching Japan was now strangely terrifying. Something had happened to me. Something terrible and irrevocable.

Poor, poor Natsuko! Why did she have to die? It was too awful. The harder I tried not to think the more I did think. Then, overwhelmed by the pity, the pity of it, I sobbed convulsively. I realized that I was not acting the man, but when memories came crowding in I simply couldn't keep my self-control.

I who had been the most happy person on the ship and the most eager to reach Japan was now the most unhappy and the least interested in getting back.

How had that come about? I wanted to die too in one swift instant, I often felt. But of course I was not one to whom death had been granted. But my heart had lost all hope. It had lost its life-giving sun.

But just then I was aware of someone sending a thin ray of love towards me. It was a humble, selfless love. Like the morning star which one scarcely notices while the sun is up, I felt it shining upon me from a great distance. It was my mother.

Until now I had almost forgotten that my mother was waiting for me. I had not actually forgotten her, but she had not been often in my thoughts. If she had been, my thoughts of Natsuko had been much stronger.

Now in the depths of my wretchedness I felt the love of my mother. She was waiting.

But as I thought of her I was reminded again of Natsuko. What a terrible thing had happened!

30

I can never set down in full detail the agonies I suffered at that time. I had aged in an instant. I was benumbed. I lacked the strength to rise. But no matter how grief-stricken I was, the ship kept advancing at a constant speed. Neither at Hongkong nor at Shanghai did I have the heart to go ashore. I did nothing but weep.

What a tragedy that I, a living person, had no power to help the dead, I thought. How could there ever be consolation for me! How she must have suffered! I had so wanted to see her. If only I could have held her hand as she breathed her last! No matter how much I thought about it nothing could be changed.

The fact that the ship was proceeding right on schedule was now driving me mad.

November 12th—that November 12th for which Natsuko had been waiting and for which I too had waited and waited finally arrived, and the ship reached Kobe on schedule and everybody was wild with excitement, but I sat vacantly in my cabin like one who had lost his mind.

Crowds of people came pouring in. I stared at them blankly. Then I saw Nonomura and my brother. Nonomura began to cry loudly and clasped my hand.

For the first time without anyone around to inhibit me, I began to sob wildly. My brother wept too.

Oh if only Natsuko were still alive! But after I had cried myself out, my heart felt somewhat eased. I got up. Then escorted like some nobleman, I stood at last on Japanese soil. They handled me as if I were a fragile thing about to break into pieces.

I did not want them to worry about me. None of us had the courage to talk about Natsuko. But we knew what was in each other's thoughts. I wanted to know how Natsuko looked in her last moments, but I knew that if I asked about her we would burst into tears again and I couldn't bring myself to do it.

"Our Mother is terribly worried, so I'm going to send her a telegram," said my brother, and he went out.

Nonomura and I remained. Finally I could no longer restrain myself and burst into sobs again.

31

They asked me if I wanted to spend the night at Kobe. I said that wouldn't be necessary. I had caused them too much trouble already and I didn't want to cause them any more. No matter how deeply they were concerned, there was nothing they could do. I wanted to hurry back to my mother who was waiting for her son's return. And then to go into my own room. And then to cry to my heart's content.

For the first time in my life I traveled first class on the train to Tokyo. Everything I saw and heard reminded me of Natsuko, but my mind was already exhausted. Somehow the feeling of being back in Japan and being pitied gave me a measure of calmness. Saying that I was sleepy, I turned my head. Soon

I was dozing away. They had been very good to me. I was very grateful.

The train arrived at Tokyo Station. My sister-in-law and Nonomura's wife were there to meet me.

"We bid you welcome," said my sister-in-law with a faint smile. I too managed a smile. It was a bit forced. But thanks to it, I kept from crying.

When I got home my mother met me at the entrance. "It's good to see you again," she said. Then she burst into tears. They seemed to be tears of gladness. Then I was filled with grief again. If only Natsuko were still alive, I felt with a fresh poignancy. It is such an awful thing to die. How could such an irrevocable thing happen to her, I asked myself with a feeling of loneliness that chilled me to the bone.

I wept for a while. Someone came to the door of my room. My mother's voice said, "Dinner is ready and everybody is waiting. Won't you come now?" It was already about 10:30 p.m.

"I'm coming now," I said blowing my nose and wiping my eyes, and with a tear-stained face I went out to take some food. A modest feast in celebration of my return had been prepared. I had much too heavy a heart to play the part of a happy son at a dinner in honor of his return, but I was determined not to cry any more.

32

The only thing I was able to ask about that night was the location of her grave. I was told that she was buried in the Nonomura family cemetery in Taninaka. Immediately after breakfast the next morning I hurried out alone to Taninaka to find her grave. I learned where it was from a man in a tea shop where I bought some flowers.

There on a fresh tombstone was engraved not "Natsuko Muraoka" but "Natsuko Nonomura." This was too much to endure. I thought of how she had signed her last letter with the tiny characters prematurely proclaiming herself my wife. It was too much.

I laid the flowers down and bowed my head. Beneath the tombstone was the urn containing her ashes. They were all that was left of her in this world.

I tried to force myself to leave. Then Nonomura appeared. "I dropped in to see you and finding you out came straight over here," he said.

"Poor sad thing!" he exclaimed, sprinkling water over the tombstone.

We both wept.

"It's all right to let ourselves go out here," Nonomura said.

"I never, never dreamed that a thing like this could happen," I said. We both wept shamelessly and without thought of appearances.

"She was always so healthy, how could a little thing like a cold finish her? But this terrible Spanish flu thing seems to be taking only the healthy ones. How tragically cruel and senseless!" Nomura exclaimed, and then, as if to himself, continued, "Natchan never realized that she was going to die. Even in her greatest suffering she thought she would soon be well. 'I'm not going to die now,' she said to me. 'I won't die without seeing Muraoka-san. Don't worry, Brother dear, I'm not going to die. I certainly won't die.' Another time she said, 'If I die now it wouldn't be fair to Muraoka-san.' And she kept repeating, 'I've got to see Muraoka-san. I'll see him soon, won't I?' Then for a short time her condition was better and she became rather animated. 'I feel fine now,' she said, 'I'm so happy!' But the end came soon after. She said something but I couldn't make out what it was. She had a peaceful look on her face at the moment of death. I thought there was something celestial in it."

Nonomura was no longer weeping.

"I couldn't help being deeply sorry for my little sister. But upon reflecting that when a human being is dead he is finally at rest, I am consoled. I feel in my heart that my sister has become a heavenly spirit. No matter how deep my grief was I could never communicate it to her. It's really the living who are to be pitied: the dead one is released from every pain. These reflections have made me realize that my sister is neither unhappy nor pitiable. But I must admit that I sometimes get both angry and sad when I ask myself why human beings are subject to such a stupid thing as death. This, however, is the living person's, not the dead one's, way of thinking," Nonomura concluded emphatically, "and so I believe now that we should no longer grieve for my sister."

"What you say is true enough. But the fact remains that I can't keep myself from grieving terribly over Natsuko," I replied.

"True enough, but that's because you're still a living creature," Nonomura insisted. Nevertheless, my heart was not consoled by his words.

Nonomura asked if I wouldn't come home with him, but I had no desire to suffer a harder blow than any yet.

I returned to my own house. The feeling of loneliness, of irreparable loss, of a wretchedness from which I could never escape, kept growing in me and trampling down my spirit.

Thus prostrated with grief, I was in a state of barely being alive.

33

One day a young friend called on me and said, "I'm thinking of giving a welcome-home party for you. What do you think of the idea?"

"Please, not just now!"

"Nonomura-san suggested that we might have it a little later, but at your farewell party we promised you a welcome-home party at Nonomura's on your return, and we're all eager to carry out that promise."

"At Nonomura's!" I exclaimed, shocked at their failure to understand what my nerves had undergone, but I suddenly reflected that if Natsuko had a soul and if the party were held at Nonomura's she would also be present there to welcome me. And so, despite the many painful memories associated with the place, I gave my consent.

Afterward it struck me that I must have been in a rather peculiar frame of mind when I gave my consent. Actually, I had been in a sort of defiant mood.

I had felt an urge to fight that cruel Nature which had killed Natsuko and was now making threatening faces at me. I had resolved not to show my back to the enemy.

It became impossible for me to sit still. Whenever I tried to I was overwhelmed by loneliness. I alternated between reading books feverishly and wandering around aimlessly.

After having been away from Japan traveling in the West for even a short while, how comforting it was to walk in places where one saw only Japanese.

Being a person given to reflection even when in a foreign land, I walked around lost in thought and sometimes I forgot that I had ever been away from Japan. The image of Natsuko was always with me on my walks. Suddenly some sixth sense would give me the sensation that someone was watching me.

Looking around then for the first time, I would have the feeling of being in the midst of a strange race—a solitary yellow face with a flat nose and black hair wearing ill-fitting Western style clothes. Everybody's eyes on me! Unable to keep my shoulders back! Never felt such nervousness in Japan! Never experienced this while walking in Japan. Only Japanese there! A quiet, soothing place to be!

But then Natsuko's face would suddenly float before my eyes. In spite of my efforts to keep from thinking about her, I couldn't help doing so. No matter where I happened to be then, whether on the street or elsewhere, I would feel an overwhelming urge to cry. Then in great anguish I would hurry home.

A few days after my friend's visit, Nonomura came and said with a look of surprise, "There's some talk about a welcome-home party for you at my place. Is it true that you agreed to it?"

"If it won't disturb you to have it at your place, I will think of it as a memorial gathering, and I have the feeling somehow that Natsuko's soul will be present."

"If that's how you look at it, I approve, but when I first heard the matter discussed I was surprised, and I thought I'd better see you about it."

"I still feel terribly crushed. Somehow I have a growing feeling of loneliness and of not being able to sit or stand still. But I am going to fight it. I will not give in to it."

"I'm glad to hear you say that. If Natsuko does have a soul, she will certainly be delighted."

"I feel that she will help me," I said.

Although even now when I am in a reflective mood and the memories come flooding in I burst into tears, these outbursts kept decreasing and gradually my appetite came back. I have never recovered completely from the blow of Natsuko's death, but I think I can say that I have become somewhat reconciled to it.

But I can't deny that I have felt at times that I might go mad from the feeling of eternal loneliness enveloping me in ten-fold, yes twenty-fold layers.

The day of the welcome-home party finally arrived.

34

But I must not fail to tell about the time shortly before then when I visited Nonomura's home and first entered Natsuko's room. The room looked just as it always had. I was afraid to go in. I was aware that if I did I would never be able to hold back my grief. But not to go in was out of the question. Nonomura himself suggested that maybe I had better wait. But I simply had to go in. Then I asked Nonomura if I might go in alone. I went in trembling. Then I closed the door. It was a Western-style room. Containing myself as well as I could, I looked around the room calmly. My picture was where it always had been. The picture of myself in front of Notre Dame Cathedral was hanging above the desk, and below it was a sheet of paper with some 180 circles of which all but 18 had been crossed out. When I saw this, the grief which I was struggling to hold back burst out all at once.

I sat down in Natsuko's chair, buried my face in my hands on Natsuko's desk, and sobbed. When I had cried myself out, I seemed to hear Natsuko whispering, "Dear Boy, don't weep so bitterly over me. Please be more cheerful."

"I will be cheerful! I will be cheerful!" I exclaimed from the bottom of my heart, but then I added, "To ask me to be cheerful with you gone is just too much."

"You musn't talk like that!" I seemed to hear the same voice say.

Finished weeping at last, I got up and looked around the room again. The way the room looked when she was still alive was vividly before my eyes. Here she wrote her letters to me, read my letters to her, and turned somersaults! My loneliness returned with fresh poignancy.

With a deep bow toward the room in general I went out. Returning to Nonomura's room, I sat down on a chair in silence. Nonomura remained silent too.

Then I said, "Anyhow I intend to fight. I'm not licked."

"I'm convinced of that. Natchan is certainly praying that you will too."

"But I feel so very lonely!"

"I know."

"No one but your mother can understand this feeling of mine."

"I am truly sorry for my mother. Still alive, her daughter dead: she is stunned by the reversal in the order of things. She says she she envies my father his having gone earlier."

Death's being wedded to life was for human beings a cruel, unnecessary thing, I thought. Especially when a splendid young person had to die.

But it was an unalterable fact, and no human being could do anything about it.

Wanting to be alone, I left Nonomura's house.

Four or five days after this experience I attended the welcome-home party.

35

When I arrived, five or six persons were already there. They were laughing and talking gaily as if without a care in the world. Seeing me, one of them said, "Congratulations!"

Two or three others said the same thing, but one or two who knew how I was feeling seemed unable to bring themselves to say it.

I became concerned that the commotion might be disturbing Nonomura's mother. So I asked Nonomura, "How is your mother?"

"She went the day before yesterday to Shizuoka Prefecture. My younger brother's wife there is going to have a baby."

"She is? Well, congratulations!"

"Mother has been saying that it could be Natsuko being born again. She had been saying for some time, though, that she hoped it would be a boy."

Hearing that, "How wonderful!" I said to myself. But then I asked myself, "Is birth such a blessing, really?"

Gradually the group became larger. Except for one person away on a trip, everybody who had been at the earlier gathering was present. Not a few persons had been carried off by the recent "Spanish flu" epidemic. Natsuko was proof of its virulence. But the faces of the rest of the group exuded health. Besides the person away on business, there was one other absent— my dearest Natsuko. But today I would not weep. I had come determined not to shed a single tear.

The meeting place was the large guest room we had met in the time before.

I could not help thinking from time to time how wonderful it would have been if Natsuko had been alive and with us. But with everybody in such high spirits, I became quite cheerful myself, and from my lips too came the sound of vacant laughter.

The food was also similar to that we had had before. Each person spoke a few words to me. I gave each a brief answer.

Finally Nonomura got up. Everybody clapped.

"It gives me pleasure to express my sincere happiness at the fact that Muraoka is safely back and that we are able to have a welcome-home party for him in the same room in which we gave him a going-away party. We have all read with interest the articles about the West that Muraoka sent to the periodicals and newspapers and have recognized Muraoka himself in them. Muraoka will no doubt express his own views on the matter, but I'm sure we all feel that he has not made this trip to the West in vain. I personally, however, feel that I owe Muraoka a very deep apology. Since this is an informal meeting and since you probably know what I'm driving at anyhow, I'm going to state bluntly that it was I who first urged Muraoka to go to the West and that Muraoka, having just become engaged to my sister Natsuko who died this fall, was reluctant to go. Not being God, I could not foresee that my sister would die while he was away, and so I told him not to worry—that I would take care of my sister for him. Yet my sister did die while he was away. I don't know how I can ever make amends to him for this. I repent deeply that I was so bold as to take such a terrible responsibility. I have wanted very much to apologize to him, but I have not been able to do so until now. No matter how depressed or how angry Muraoka becomes he never loses his self-control. He has been too kind to blame me in any way, but I want to beg forgiveness for my mistake just the same. And so I pray from the bottom of my heart that Muraoka will henceforth have good health and a persevering mind. I am certain that my sister is praying likewise. It is selfish of me to dodge my responsibility by begging Muraoka to be strong, but I make this hard request because we all expect so much from him." At this point Nonomura seemed about to break down. "I'd better stop now," he said.

The applause was thin. No one spoke a word. Then I got up. Everybody clapped.

"Nonomura-san," I said on the verge of tears, which I suppressed, however, by shifting my thoughts, "is in no way to blame. Man is born to die. No human being is immortal. I myself might die tomorrow. That is not likely to happen, but human life is fragile. That truth I have just learned well. I have learned it to the point of being angry at my having been born a human being."

As I said this I stared at my invisible foe. I spoke with the feeling that the god of death was somewhere near.

"Nothing is simpler than for the god of death to kill a human being. He doesn't even take pride in it. I have come back alive. It's not because I have any special merit that I am still alive. A good person can die too. Sometimes one does." I was again on the verge of tears, but a feeling of defiance toward something kept me rambling on incoherently. "And a worthless creature may be left alive. A person who accomplishes nothing by being alive may be permitted to live. I, a creature so sinful that I would have no right to complain if I had been doomed to die, keep living. I have never gone so far as to call myself a criminal. But in comparison with the person who has died I certainly am one. But now that I have been left alive I must do something."

Four or five persons clapped. I felt my head begin to reel.

"It's not that I'm not willing to die. But would that console the one who has died? Hardly. She doesn't need to be consoled. The god of death can kill at will any human being. But that human being then becomes a god—a being greater than any man. He is then too exalted to be consoled by mere human beings. He has become too blessed, much too blessed a god. God of death, I say to you, you may have the power to kill human beings, but you are really only a pawn for the purpose of turning men into gods. Nevertheless, even though we who remain know that only too well, we can't keep from grieving over the person who has died. This is blunt talk, but it's the truth. But there's nothing I can do to help her any more. What I can do is work for the living. There are so many wretched people on the earth. Yes, human beings are without exception wretched creatures until they die. Every last one is a wretched thing. I have traveled in the West. There were nothing but wretched beings everywhere. I doubt whether there is a single real philosopher anywhere.

("If there is," I had an insane impulse to say, "he stands here before you.")

"But human beings are hardly aware of their wretchedness. I wasn't. In my happiness I could hardly wait to get back to Japan. Naturally enough. We forget that we ourselves are moving toward death, and that is proof of our health. But we cannot help being aware that we are wretched. When I went to the West I saw all sorts of things but I didn't learn anything new. Human beings are the same everywhere. About all I learned is that there are other people besides the Japanese. But just before reaching Hong Kong a single telegram made me turn a somersault. Yes, a somersault! My life was turned upside-down. The cherry blossom world of spring was suddenly transformed into the icy world of winter. Even greater was the change in me. Indeed, it was enough to bring me to the thin line between life and death. I do not expect anything ever to be born of that. I still feel a blind anger at what has happened. But none toward any human being. Nonomura-san cannot help being stunned by the loss of the sister he loved so dearly. Her mother is even more stunned. I don't want to talk about myself. But I am trying to think of a way to avenge myself against this terribly cruel fate. The slain person becomes a god. No revenge is as sweet as that. For myself there will be no revenge as sweet as that, but no matter how many times I am knocked down I will always get up again and bow to Natsuko-san's love and her spirit. Nevertheless, the realization that in doing so I will not be able to comfort Natsuko-san or give her any pleasure at all, gives me a certain feeling of sadness."

At this point I suddenly stopped talking, bowed, and sat down.

Everybody clapped. Suddenly I got up and left the room. I ran into Natsuko's room, and, throwing myself onto Natsuko's desk, wept to my heart's content.

How long I remained there, I don't know. Finally I managed to regain self-possession and returned to my seat. The group greeted my return with silence. But I was able to sense in the breathless hush how eager everybody was to impart strength to me. Full of gratitude to my friends for their solicitude, I sat down.

36

This is something that happened 21 years ago.

But it hasn't lost its vividness in my memory even now. I still believe that the human being is a frail, pitiful thing.

I feel it a great pity that the person who has died is able to wield great power over the living whereas a living person is absolutely powerless to affect the one who has died.

Even now I can't stop grieving a great deal over Natsuko's death. But the conviction that the departed is too blessed and too god-like to need the help of the living is for me at least a great consolation.

Is any other attitude possible?